MOVING ON

J.L. Caban

ISBN: 978-1-7369996-6-0

Rare Jewels Literary Works

Table of Contents

ONE 9

TWO 16

THREE 22

FOUR 29

FIVE 33

SIX 35

SEVEN 43

EIGHT 47

NINE 51

TEN 57

ELEVEN 63

TWELVE 72

THIRTEEN 76

FOURTEEN 79

FIFTEEN 84

SIXTEEN 91

SEVENTEEN 95

EIGHTEEN 99

NINETEEN 104

TWENTY 107

TWENTY ONE 110

NOTE FROM THE AUTHOR

I recently had an epiphany. The proverbial light bulb illuminated above my head as I was looking through some of my old college papers and the unfinished stories that I had written when I was between eighteen and nineteen years old; this book being one of them. At the time, I had a great interest in becoming a writer. I declared myself an English major at Lehman College, a charming oasis in the middle of the sultry borough of the Bronx, New York, and had dreams - more like delusions of grandeur - of becoming a renowned writer of fiction.

I've always had a great love for reading the works of the 'giants' of the literary world, such as Melville, Dumas, Hemingway, Wharton, Austen, and my favorite, Salinger (not that I dare - for a single solitary second - place myself within a universe's distance of these iconic artists of prose). As I would read these timeless classics, I would often fantasize about actually creating something of my own; but sometimes life's twists and turns take you in a different direction.

Somewhere along my collegiate journey, I had a change of heart and decided to change my major, which led to my receiving a Bachelor of Arts in Psychology and a Master of Science in Education. It wasn't until I serendipitously stumbled across my 'coming of age' story, as it were, Moving On, that had been laying dormant inside of my desk drawer for years (twenty-eight years later to be exact) that the fiery passion for writing was reignited. After unearthing my old work, and with the strength given to me by God, I went to work resurrecting this book.

Now, the question was, did I want to adjust and amend the timeline of the story to bring it into the present day? Would it ruin the innocence, authenticity and integrity of the characters? Would it completely distort the events as they originally were written? I decided that I would not alter the timeline set forth twenty-eight years ago; therefore, I humbly request the reader to keep in mind that this story takes place in the early 1990s, a different time. It was the last decade of the 20th century and the Zeitgeist - spirit of the time - was much more relaxed than the chaotic times of now and the mind frame of people as whole was more tolerant, so to speak. It was a decade in which almost everyone was on the 'same page' in regards to fashion, music and interest in the arts in general. Another thing that the reader should keep in mind, something that is essential in order to understand the work, is that this time period was very 'behind' as compared to the present era in regards to technology. For instance, during the story, you may ask yourself, 'Why doesn't the protagonist just use his cell phone? Why is he using a pay phone?' Well, the reason for that would be, in the 1990s, cell phones were not as prevalent. People of that time period would walk around with 'loose change' - a plethora of mixed coins (quarters, nickels, dimes &c.) and use public pay phones to make phone calls, if they weren't home. If a person was inside their home, they would then use an antiquated landline which was plugged into an electrical outlet. This barbaric method of telecommunication would relegate one to a small perimeter, as the cord connected to the telephone was limited in length. People left messages on answering machines, which were connected to the landline phones, and one could either call their home phone from yet another phone elsewhere - where ever they happened to be - and enter a code to retrieve these messages, or simply wait until they arrived at home to listen to the messages. Yes, I know, dear reader, this was very archaic!

Our protagonist, Justin Christianson, whom you will meet shortly, is both spiritually and mentally lost; however, he has a humanistic thirst for redemption and wants desperately to understand and immerse himself in the goings on of the people with whom he is acquainted - people who are essentially 'moving on' with their own lives; however, he has absolutely no idea how to accomplish this, nor does he understand that he himself is the key to solving this enigma. His girlfriend, Judith Cardinal, is more like a proverbial crutch - a security blanket - than a romantic companion and if she were removed from his world, it would send him plummeting to a morbid state of despair; not for the loss of her per say, but more because of his fear of bitter loneliness as well as the unknown, although during his story, he is quite unaware of this fact. Somehow, someway, he must take hold of his life and reach his fullest potential; he must become a self sustaining, productive member of society and leave behind, once and for all, the world of drugs and alcohol (his other crutch) and the inability to self love that has kept him in the dark for so long.

Now, grab a glass of wine (or a glass of cider, depending on your age!), place some cheese and extra virgin olive oil on a cracker, find a cozy nook and enjoy my tale of a young man who, like the Phoenix, rises from the ashes of his world filled with hopelessness and despair and begins to search his soul, so that he too - like all adolescents before him - can complete his rite of passage and find his place in the world.

DEDICATION

For my wife

Cecilia

For my father and mother

Joe & Lisa

For my brother

Ivan

For my children

Ashley

Jesiah

Joey

Julian

I was pretty sure, at that point, around June of 1990, I should have been sitting in a padded room, wrapped up in a white straitjacket, rocking back and forth and salivating thick saliva from my mouth, the kind that seems to be able to withstand the fiercest tornadoes and hurricanes. The kind that never breaks. I'm pretty sure that's where I should've been. I had come to a point in my life where my last screw had come loose. There wasn't a rational bone in my entire frail body. I was quite frail. I'm about five-foot-ten, I weighed something close to a hundred and twenty pounds and at the time I was eighteen years old (I'm nineteen, now). That made me at least forty pounds underweight, which is something I can't understand, being that I am the greediest pig (when it comes down to eating) in the whole miserable world. I mean it, I'm a real hog. I've been known to nab food from people's plates without a single shred of shame. I, however, do not gain a single stupid pound. My father, the guy I live with, whom I will tell you about later, says that I have a fast metabolism. Ever since he's been keeping up with his health, he feels it necessary to comment on my well-being now and then.

The one thing I do have going for me, the one thing I really adore about myself, is my looks. I'm a real fox, I have to admit. I've got these really exotic hazel-gray eyes, a thick, sexy pair of eyebrows, and a fabulous hairdo, sort of like Elvis' hair - the young Elvis, not the old fat guy with the huge sideburns and bedazzled jumpsuit. I also have a hell of a facial structure. I've got a chiseled chin, strong jawline and an aquiline nose; you know, the type of features that those gorgeous male models from Calvin Klein have, like the one that has his picture on that building downtown in the Village, Marky Mark I think his name is. As a matter of fact, I could have been a stupid model. I just never got around to signing up, that's all. They make you sign up for that kind of stuff and who in the hell has time for that? Not me. The auditions; the rejections; the long lines of guys who look the same, dress the same, practicing their best puckered lip facial expression, waiting to be seen by some rat-fink agent who is ready to have you sell your soul to the Prince of the Underworld; no thank you. Anyway, before I lose myself, let me tell you how I arrived at such a morbidly bleak and hopeless state of affairs.

It pretty much started the day I decided to get myself together by getting off drugs and alcohol. In the not too distant past, I was in some basement half the time, sniffing my damn nostrils away on cocaine, smoking marijuana and getting boozed up on malt liquor, also known as 'liquid crack'; it really was like consuming the drug known as crack, except in the form of a thick brown liquid. Very appetizing, I know. The reason, if you ask me why I did any of that, isn't some major, nail biting, edge of your seat tale. It's simply because I fell in with the wrong crowd. I hung out with some really seedy people that did some really shitty things (things that I probably shouldn't mention because they'd most likely get really upset with me if I did). Anyway, my girlfriend - more like my champion, my salvation - at the time, Judith Cardinal, helped me to get away from all of that crap. She was really good to me, nursing me to health during those really horrific withdrawal periods; keeping me from relapsing; not allowing me to associate with the washouts that I hung out with while doing my dirty business. I'll tell you more about her later on, too. In the meantime, I'll tell you how I went back to school to get my equivalency diploma and all after dropping out of high school having completed my junior year, but not quite ever starting my senior year (unless you count hanging out just outside the high school, Columbus High School, in the Bronx, with the other truants while everyone else in the world was inside attending class).

Once I got into the wonderful world of drugs and drinking, I never really spent any time with the outside world, and I wasn't used to dealing with 'normal' everyday people. The thing is, they were all around me now. I have to tell you, I didn't like it one single bit. It was pretty horrifying having to assimilate and conform to blend back into society. I never knew - I never imagined - how pathetic and truly frightening people really are. I mean, they're absolutely diabolical, not to mention completely insane. People. They act like animals and don't care about anyone but themselves. For example, take rush hour down at Forty-Second Street, Grand Central Station in New York City. I have seen people push and leap - yes, leap like an Olympic track star - over someone else to get a seat on the train. Subsequently, the person feels he must break a few of your ribs while sitting next to you fighting for elbow space; and, after essentially shattering every part of your skeleton, they have the unmitigated gall to get angry at you for not being absolutely in love with them for doing so. I swear it, people are all complete sociopaths.

I went to night classes in the summer of 1990 to get my crazy GED at City College in Manhattan, New York City. The classes began the first week of June; they started at 6:00 PM and ended at around 9:00 PM. For anyone that does or ever did live or have any other reason to be around City College, which is on Convent Avenue, between 141st Street and 145th Street in Harlem, New York, you know that night time isn't exactly the greatest time to be out (except, of course, if you are wearing the right gang color and know the secret hand signal and are perhaps 'packing heat'). Once you got to the campus, though, it wasn't so bad. It was actually quite beautiful, what with the plush trees, green grass and all that kind of crap. It's just the area around the school that gave me the creeps, filled with crackheads, transvestite prostitutes, and other glorious, productive members of society's elite class. I had no choice but to go to school at that time because they only offered the GED classes at night. I suppose they did that to see who was really devoted to getting their diploma, who knows. I mean, if you somehow found the will and courage to bypass all of the scum of the earth to get to the campus, you really must want to attend these classes. Don't get me wrong, I'm sure there were some really decent, hard working people around there somewhere. I'm just telling you what I saw, that's all.

I wound up in a classroom full of former drug dealers and prostitutes, bored husbands and wives, and freshly arrived immigrants from third world nations. I went straight to the back of the classroom where I was conditioned into sitting during my three and a half years of high school (I used to sit in the back, so that I could fall asleep all over my desk during class at Columbus).

While waiting for the GED teacher to show up, I had the misfortune of hearing some of the lost souls and degenerates having discussions amongst themselves. "What in da hell we gonna learn today?" Some guy with a patch over his eye and a few missing teeth yelled to his slow-witted crony, who donned a neon yellow baseball cap with the words, 'Real Men Eat Ass' printed on the front. Very high class.

"What I look like, da friggin teacha?" Was the eloquent reply.

"Yo, you da one who done been here three times already. You should be knowin all dat shit, mutha fucka."

"Why you tryin ta 'barass me fronna all deez people? I should come ova dare and knock da resta yo teef out."

"I'm just playin, don't be a little bitch about it, yo."

Ah, the scholastic life; so refreshing. I got a migraine from that conversation real fast. I tried to focus in on another one to flush the taste of disgust from the former.

"Does Loretta like you being here?" One pretty decent looking guy with a very handsome pink and white striped Ralph Lauren buttoned down shirt asked another well behaved looking gentleman.

"Fuck that whore."

There went that. The disgruntled gentleman continued, "That two timin' trick probably doesn't even notice I'm gone. I'm telling you, Jack, she's got it in for me. I caught her dancing all over the house, humming tunes from that Julio Iglesias album. She never did that before."

"Maybe she's just in a good mood, Dave. That happens to women sometimes. It's their biological clock. I read all about it in this Hustler Magazine while I was on the shitter at Al's Strip and Sip the other night."

"Their clock?! What in the hell does the time have to do with -"

Just then, just before I slit both my wrists, the teacher waltzed in. She wasn't what you would call a traditionally handsome woman. She had a major acne situation going on and from what she was wearing, you could see she had a decent sized gut, kind of like she was smuggling a few medium to large sized items out of the local dollar store under the bottom of her shirt. Compared to the other trolls in the classroom, though, she was a goddess. She had long, blonde hair (dyed) with black streaks emanating from the roots, which cascaded down her scalp onto her linebacker-type shoulders, and decent sized boobs, which she was exploiting with her very sheer, violet colored, low cut, v-neck blouse.

"Hello, everyone!" Her voice was about an octave away from shattering everyone's eardrum into a million little pieces. She had a voice that practically only dogs could detect. "My name is Sweet Sue. Sweet is an a-d-j-e-c-t-i-v-e." Sue was speaking to us as though we were in a kindergarten class, where the kids are squatting on a rug, getting ready for story-time, which was insane because the average age of the classroom was about thirty-five. The human dog whistle continued, "I want all of you to pick an adjective to go along with your names, okay? It's a fun little way to get to know all of you!" She squeaked, as the entire classroom was now completely mesmerized and dumbfounded as to what was happening. She pointed her crooked finger to the side of the classroom closest to the window and said, "We'll start with this side of the room, then we'll work our way around to this side" (the door side). "You first. What shall we call you?" She was aiming her dislocated, witch-like, pointer finger at this ancient, old, Indian woman, about in her late thirties, who had no idea what in the hell was going on.

The old lady looked as though she had been shot with a damn stun gun. "I am being sorry," She said in a thick Indian accent. "I am not knowing of this procedure. Kindly explain."

"Well, an adjective is something that describes a person, place, or thing. For example, I'm Sweet Sue, now who are you?" Sue said in this kind of poetic verse that made me want to vomit all over the place.

"I am being Adelphi."

"Okay, Adelphi, now pick an adjective to go along with your name. You know, Adoring Adelphi, Alluring Adelphi, and so on." Sue was losing her cool and her spunky spirit. Little beads of sweat were beginning to form just over her uni-brow. I don't think she prepared herself for this debacle.

They stared at each other for approximately twenty seconds when good ol' Adelphi's light bulb went on - bless her heart. She came up with a name and, with a gleaming look of pride and the utmost confidence, said, "Aldephi the Bus! I love to the bus, so I am the bus."

As Adelphi awaited approval from Sweet Sue, amidst a fraction of a second of deafening silence, the class finally let out a thunderous laugh so loud that I was sure all their lungs would projectile out of their mouths and noses and end up all over the floor. Not me, though. I sort of felt sorry for ol' Adelpi, who was very confused at the reaction of the class and still standing by for approval. Sue didn't give her any, though. She just skipped on over to the next person. "Next."

She went through the whole class until she finally came to me. I don't mind saying that I really didn't want to do this crap. It was crazy. What was all this for anyway? It was bad enough I had to be in this room with these rejects of humanity, but now I had to play idiotic children's games with them, too. I pulled myself together and thought of Judith, the only reason I was in this place. She insisted I get an education because I'd need it in the future. I put on this tough guy look, so that the drug dealers and other low life individuals in the class wouldn't think I was some kind of flake. I mean, they all picked names like Robbing Randy and Looting Larry. What in the hell was I supposed to pick?

Then it happened. The thing that happens to people when they're not ready to speak up, but are suddenly forced. "Jolly Justin." I said. The funny thing is, it kind of spilled out of my mouth in slow motion. I could even see the words practically dripping out of my mouth, slowly, like molasses oozing down the bark of a tree.

"Jolly Justin, that's so cute!" Sue chimed in. "Isn't that cute everyone?" Sweet Sue was making it worse. She was really drilling it in now. Really laying it on thick. "Now that's a perfect example of a synonym! And so very sweet!" She said, giving me a smile and a wink.

Robbing Randy and Looting Larry just gave me this look like I was a couple of layers of dog shit. "What is this guy, some kinda fruit?" One of them whispered. They both looked at me like I was going to get a major beat down after class. I averted their menacing stares by turning my head towards the window, wishing with all my heart and soul that I was on the other side of it.

As the hours trudged along, I started glancing around the class and, at one point, I locked eyes with Ol' Adelphi, who sort of gave me this tilted head, motherly smile. Everybody else, thank God, was already fast asleep. I lay back in my seat as far back as I possibly could, face flushed, and thought of about a thousand places I'd rather be. I noticed the clock atop of the doorway and stared at the hands, counting every agonizing second for the remainder of the night.

TWO

Class was over at around nine in the evening, but I decided to walk around the inside of the building for a bit. There was something very compelling about being inside there. The walls were made of dark wood that smelled of old pine, very stimulating to the ol' senses. What I liked, too, was that the floor was also made of an aged hardwood, which made a creaking sound as you walked along. There were these really interesting framed portraits of years ago along the hallway walls. The photos were of City College students from like the 1930s all the way through to the present, but I found the older ones way more fascinating. I gazed at the images and wondered where all those people were now and what they were doing with themselves. Were any of them like me, lost and unsure about themselves? Were they happy with their lives now? Were they even still alive? I find that stuff very intriguing. I love looking at old photographs; looking deep into the eyes of the people and just fantasizing about their lives and what it must've been like for them. Sometimes, if you really focus on a person in a snapshot, you can connect with them in a way. Like they start to almost speak to you. It's pretty deep stuff.

Anyway, I got so lost in looking at the pictures, that I didn't realize how much time had gone by. It was about nine forty-five when I finally got outside, it was pretty late. It was a very humid June evening and there was no moon in the sky, so it was insanely dark outside. I didn't have a chance to get a feel for the campus before I got to class, so I was as good as lost in that place. The lighting wasn't all that spectacular either due to the fact that they had these very dim street lamps that barely lit up the walkways, so it's not like I could see my stupid hand in front of my face or anything like that. I figured if I started walking around, I'd get the hell out of there by the end of the century. What I found truly amazing was, out of the thirty damn people in my class, there wasn't a single bastard in sight. Not one miserable soul. I was getting a little nervous if you want to know the truth. City College didn't have dorms; so, people cleared the hell out of there at about nine-thirty in the evening. I seriously didn't think I'd see civilization ever again. I get frightened pretty easily, especially of the dark. I'm a huge believer in spirits and lost souls that wander the earth, so I'm always looking over my shoulder to make sure there aren't any ghouls and goblins sneaking up on me whenever I'm in places which lack illumination.

To be honest, I got this phobia from my mother. It was one of the things she most generously passed to me as a child before she took off (she left my dad and I when I was in the third grade, although I still keep in touch with her, which I'll share with you later). She, in my presence, used to pretend to talk to spirits in the dark, which I don't mind telling you scared the living hell out of me. She even described them in detail; the way they looked, what they were wearing and all of their various gripes that made them very upset, especially if I was misbehaving, which was supposed to make me stop acting the fool; but all it did - all it managed to do - was give me an unreasonable and very humiliating fear of the afterlife and of the dark in general. Thanks mom.

Anyway, ready to accept defeat and give up all hope of ever finding the exit to the campus, I began looking around for a soft spot to set up camp and go the hell to sleep. Out of the darkness, a silhouette appeared from between the trees; I thought for sure that it must have been the infamous creature my mother taunted me about all those years ago. I stood frozen, awaiting the end, ready to meet my maker, when the shadowy figure came into the light. It wasn't - to my relief - a monster. It was City College's finest. Out from the mist, shining a flashlight brighter than a million suns combined, came this guy with one of those fake police uniforms which came complete with a square badge that resembled the small toys that you get for a quarter in those supermarket machines by the check-out register.

He probably figured I was trying to rob the joint because he started yelling at me. "Hey slim, where do you think you're going?" He was shining that damn spot light on me, which made these little green stars flash before my eyes. He was pretty huge; as in, extremely obese. His uniform shirt was half untucked with remnants of some sort of extremely old cheese sauce that, at one point in his career, must have dribbled from his mouth down onto the buttons - two of which, incidentally, were missing - and the cap device on his hat was aslope. A real display of authority and professionalism, I must say.

I think it was for that reason that I answered back with an attitude. I mean, here's a guy that, without that shameful, appallingly sloppy uniform, probably gets called every insulting name in the book; but, the minute he puts on that Halloween costume, though, he figures he can go yell at somebody. People are morons. "I'm not going anywhere. I'm just standing here looking stupid. You know, for kicks." I was pretty sarcastic for someone who was lost in the dark.

I waited, expecting a back hand slap from the fuzz. He just stood there, moving his flashlight up and down, giving me the once over. "Listen, pal," I wasn't his damn pal. I hate when people call you pal when they know damn well they're not your pal. Especially when, under no circumstances whatsoever, would we ever be anything remotely close to pals. "I wouldn't get smart if I was you, slim. You ain't supposed to be here. This here is private property and yooze trespassin'. Campus closed ten minutes ago, so now I'm gonna ax you again, where do you think yer goin'?" For emphasis, he poked my chest in rhythmic unison to every syllable with his extremely oversized flashlight which, by the way, would have given Sigmund Freud a wet dream.

That's where I got off the macho train. I sort of had to be realistic. He was at least five hundred pounds heavier than me and I didn't exactly have the territorial or tactical advantage, either. I changed my tune at that point and with the utmost humility, I answered, "I take GED classes here. I was trying to find the exit to the damn place, but I got lost. I couldn't find my way out."

You could tell he was going over my story really hard because he had his mouth tilted sideways and one of his eyebrows was lifted up like he was trying to push out an obstinate pocket of air from his asshole. I'm telling you, the wheels were really turning. "So, why was you walking around here for?"

Was he serious? I don't know, maybe I didn't make myself clear. I thought I just finished telling this ignoramus that I was lost. "I'm lost." I repeated. "I lost my way when I came out of the building."

He made that stupid face again. The thinking face. "You got proof yooze in dat GDP class?" This guy was the pits.

I let the error slide and began sifting through my jean jacket pockets for the admission card they gave me to take the class; however, I couldn't find it. I'm sure there are a few of you out there who can relate to this; whenever I'm looking for something and I really need to find it, it grows legs and gets lost. What is it with that? I mean, really.

"I'm waiting, son. Let's have it." This guy had to be pretty lonely for me to have been his 'pal' and 'son' all in one night.

"It's here. I just have to find it." I searched everywhere. My pants pocket, jacket pocket, book bag, the floor around me, the sky above me; I had lost it.

I continued to stall for a few more seconds, but good ol' Andy Griffith had seen enough. He took hold of my arm real hard and started leading me toward the dark, black hole in which he appeared. "C'mon, I'm taking you to the command center! You can tell the rest of your story to the head of security!"

Oh boy, I was going to meet the one and only head of City College security. To think, some people don't have it this good. It was going to be like meeting the Wonderful Wizard of Oz, I'm sure.

The master headquarters was actually a tiny watch booth that barely fit one person. It was about a hundred and fifty degrees in that little hut and it reeked of stale fart and chili fries. Evidence of the latter was all over the shirt and pants of the wizard; the commander of the morons, the head of security.

He was about a hundred and fifty six years old, almost no hair (except for the rogue strands coming out of his nostrils and ear holes) and about three or four hundred pounds heavier than my 'pal' and 'father,' the patrolman.

"I caught this kid walkin' around the place, Jerry." The patrolman said to Jerry, the head guy.

Jerry gave me the once over. "C'mere, son." There it was again; 'son.' My mother was obviously a whore. What the hell was it with that son bullshit? "Sit down over here." He motioned toward this dilapidated chair that barely stood next to him. Seeing as how it was late, about a quarter to ten, and I was hungry and tired, I did as he told me. When I sat down, the poor chair whistled out of the hundreds of holes it possessed. "Now, what seems to be the problem, Phil?" He asked Phil, the patrolman.

"I caught this mutt walking around the campus. He says he's from some GTT class they givin' here. When I axed him for proof, he ain't have it."

"What in the hell is a GDD class?" said Jerry.

I had to jump in. "That's GED. It stands for General Educational Development." I corrected the morons.

After staring at me for about two days, Jerry, moron number two, said, "Well, so you have any proof?"

What did I do to deserve being in this hell hole with the world's biggest idiots? Didn't Phil just tell him I 'aint' have it? God help me. "I don't have it with me. I must have dropped it or something." I said, with the utmost patience. I really did have patience with these guys. I think that it had something to do with my sympathy towards individuals with mental disorders. I have this soft spot for them. I really do. Most of the time it's not their fault. It's in the genes, passed down from generations upon generations of other morons. I read that somewhere in a very credible publication, you can go check for yourself.

Jerry gave me this cross look and started tapping a pen on his desk and bopping his head to the beat he was creating. You could tell he was really knocking himself out with his musical composition, like he was ready to take it to the next level, possibly go out for an audition on Star Search and dazzle the pants off of Ed McMahon. Although I didn't know the tune he was drumming, I'm pretty sure he was off. "I'm a nice guy," (Yea, I'm sure) "so, I'm gonna let you slide this time; but, so help me, if I catch you on this campus again without ID, your ass is mine, you hear?"

I'll bet that made his day. I'm willing to bet that he's been waiting to say that line all his miserable life. Give somebody what looks like a police uniform and a wooden stick they can twirl around while walking the beat, and the first chance they get they'll tell somebody 'your ass is mine.' I nodded for sake of argument because I really wanted to get out of Dodge.

"Okay then, scoot." He gave me this stupid fatherly kind of smile. The one that fathers give after they've just finished scolding you.

I started for the door when I heard him call out, "Remember what I told you, boy!" I hate that. I hate when someone finishes giving you a lecture and says, 'remember what I said' as if I'm going to remember just because they told me to. What I am going to remember is the traumatic event of having to smell Jerry's halitosis, which reeked of a couple of spoiled cans of sardines left out in the sun for about seven weeks.

I was glad to be back outside again where the freshly polluted New York City air hung like a line of clothing that dangles for weeks outside the windows of a tenement building. The security booth was alongside the front gate, so I made it out without a problem. I couldn't wait to get the hell out of there and go home. Even though home was no family picnic, either.

THREE

I suppose now is a good time to stop and tell you about my father, Louie Christianson. There isn't much to tell, if you really want to know the truth. What I mean is, I hardly know the guy myself. Besides the fact that he's a giant (about six foot one), with dark brown hair and eyes, which sometimes makes me wonder if I really am his son, I hardly know him. We, my father and I, have lived under the same roof together for nearly nineteen years; however neither he nor I had much of an interest in each other's lives. What I do know, what was told to me by his wife - my mother - was that he supposedly had a very tough row to hoe kind of life. Apparently, he grew up on the mean streets of Spanish Harlem, New York City, running with gangs, selling drugs, and other shenanigans that got him locked up for a couple of years when he was about eighteen years old. He was a hustler of sorts until he met my mother, Laura Christianson (that's her name), who was able to subdue his criminalistic behavior; they met when he was about twenty-one and she was nineteen. According to family folklore, my dad didn't receive a tremendous amount of love or affection growing up because there wasn't anybody around to give it. His parents, which would, I suppose, make them my grandparents, were absentees. I've never met them and I'm pretty sure my dad can say the same. I guess that's why he kind of has no feelings; he's kind of an aloof dude.

My mother, the more convincing parent when it comes to genetics (she's about five foot eight with hazel eyes and light brown hair), has been living in Georgia for the past ten years because, as I mentioned earlier, she took off on me and my father years ago (when I was around eight years old). She took off like a thief in the night because - according to her version of things - he liked playing around her back. He cheated on her quite a few times with some really cute red-head named Tammy. I never thought anything of it because they, Tammy and my dad, were so open about the whole thing in front of me. They wouldn't go full on animalistic while I was around or anything, that's not what I mean. They'd just kind of hold hands and give each other innocent, but meaningful, pecks on the lips. Tammy had a daughter around my age (Clementine or Clarabelle, I can't remember which), so, this meant that half the time my attention was diverted anyway. We'd be playing together in some other area of wherever we were, so our focus was not on the extra-curricular activities going on in the adjacent rooms between our star crossed lover parents.

My mother found out, though, and decided to play his game. She began to see some guy everyday after work. Some guy named Travis. I know this because I played tag-along with her as well. I was too young to have a choice in the matter. Not too young, however, to have an opinion because, let me tell you, I'd like to have been the hell away from both my mother and father at that point. I was always in the middle of the damn thing. Both my parents gave me this speech on how the people they were seeing were, "... just friends, Justin." And also how, "... You shouldn't say anything to mommy/daddy because they wouldn't understand like you and me." What they didn't know, what the both of them didn't know, was that I didn't understand. They were too wrapped up in their own little world to realize, I guess. Maybe it made them feel better to say that stuff to me. I don't know. What I did understand was, I just wanted to be part of an ordinary home, with my mother and my father under the same roof, just being normal. I just wanted to be like all the other kids that I knew. I'd go to my friend's houses and see their parents just doing regular things. Nothing mind blowing, mind you. Nothing that you'd pay an admission fee to see. Just good old fashioned traditional stuff.

If you pointed a gun at me right now and absolutely made me explain what I mean, I'd say my friend's mom would be cooking dinner with one of those aprons that has the flowery patterns all over it, while his dad would be reading the evening newspaper, relaxing on his recliner, wearing those super comfy leather slippers with the fur inside and smoking a damn pipe filled with cherry cavendish tobacco - filling the air with that sweet, aromatic smell - while the goddamn family dog groomed himself on his doggy bed or something like that. Real cozy kind of crap; something you'd see in an episode of Leave it to

Beaver. I don't know. I used to see my friend's parents doing that sort of thing and get pretty jealous, if you want to know the absolute truth. I wondered to God why that couldn't be my life. Real cornball stuff, I know.

Anyway, when I got home that night, my father was sprawled all over the couch in his *tighty whitey* underwear and wife beater style tank-top shirt, watching Tuesday Night Fights on channel twenty-four. I could smell that the food had already been cooked; the apartment smelled of garlic and some sort of poultry. Using his peripheral vision, he addressed me. "Justin, where in the hell have you been?"

"I had GED classes tonight. I thought I mentioned that yesterday." I answered with a slight attitude. The reason being was that I was sure I mentioned it only about a million times prior; apparently it was too difficult for him to store in the old short term memory bank. I began taking off my jean jacket because it was blazing hot in the apartment. We lived in an apartment building in Pelham Parkway, the Bronx, which had no central air and my dad was too cheap to spring for an air conditioner. The temperature in that place was about the equivalent of the God forsaken Sun.

"I thought it finished at nine?" He said to the television. The fighters on the TV were in the last round with about a minute left, so they were exchanging brain ending blows in a Hail Mary effort to get a knockout, so his eyes were glued to the screen.

"It did. The bus took a long time." I really didn't feel like getting into the whole story about Jerry and the amazing time I spent inside the Earth shattering City College security stronghold. Firstly, it would've fallen on deaf ears and secondly, I hadn't eaten anything since early that morning, a grilled cheese sandwich with ovaltine - my favorite refection, and I was starving.

He accepted this farcical anecdote, probably because he didn't give a rats ass. I mean, why on God's green Earth would you pay attention to your offspring when you have two large, sweaty men brutally beating each other brain dead? Which, on this particular occasion, and to the disappointment of my father, anticlimactically, ended in a draw.

He grabbed the remote control, turned off the TV, chucked the remote across the sofa and said, "You got chicken in the oven and some potatoes on the stove. Serve yourself, I'm going to bed." With that, he peeled himself up off of the sofa and went to his room. If I haven't mentioned it already, we had an amazing relationship.

I sat in the kitchen, waiting for my food to heat up in the microwave and stared out the window down at the trees that lived ten stories below. It was a pretty captivating view consisting of a lot of plush, green vegetation. Usually, if you tell someone you're from the Bronx, they'll ask you how many times you've been a victim of some sort of violent crime; but Pelham Parkway was a pretty decent area, I have to admit. I sat and thought about whether or not to go back to those night classes. Even if I wanted to, how was I going to face ol' Jerry and his fruity sidekick, Phil, without ID? I was getting less hungry by the minute. Finally, what I did was, I dumped the chicken and potatoes in the garbage, much to the chagrin, I'm sure, of my dad when he'd see it in the trash, and made a damn grilled cheese sandwich with some ovaltine. I really didn't feel like having anything heavy and, as I already told you, I kind of have a love affair with grilled cheese and Ovaltine. I was pretty upset. I kind of felt a nervous breakdown coming on. I get those a lot. Nervous breakdowns. It's like drowning or some crazy thing like that. It's like you can't breathe and you feel like a hippopotamus is reclining on your chest, which isn't a very good feeling. I figured, at that point, I'd just have my sandwich, go the hell to sleep and put this day out of its misery.

Before I did that, before I went to bed, I decided to give Judith a ring. I was feeling pretty low and I needed her to bring my spirits up. She was seventeen, one year younger than I, and a senior at this all girls Catholic school on 56th and First Avenue called Cathedral High School, a very big deal high school. She, Judith, was very pretty. Long, light brown hair, big brown eyes, light to medium toned skin, and pretty toes, always painted and clean. There's nothing like a girl with pretty toes. It's kind of a thing with me. Don't get me wrong, I don't have a foot fetish or anything. I'm not one of those guys that wants to pour hot sauce on a girl's feet or any insane thing like that. There's just something sexy about a girl with really nice toes, that's all I'm saying. I figure, a girl that can take care of her feet can pretty much take care of all the rest of herself. That's my crazy logic, anyway and I must say it has rung true up this point.

The phone rang four whole times before she picked up, which is kind of a pet peeve of mine. Three rings maximum, that's my rule. The first ring alerts you as to the call, the second ring to collect yourself and clear your throat, and the third is the pick-up ring. Perfect system. I think it's pretty damn rude if a person lets the phone ring more than three times is the point I'm trying to drive home here. "Hello?" She said with her soothing voice that made me forgive the four ring infraction. I'm telling you, her voice could melt butter like hot popcorn.

It was almost all that I needed. I could have hung up the phone and been completely satisfied just by hearing that soft, angelic voice. I didn't, though, I didn't hang up. "Hey, it's me."

"Hey, how was your first day?" She said. She was so caring.

"Not too good. I'm not sure if I want to go back."

"What? Why? What happened?" She said, very concerned. She always sounded so concerned whenever I had unpleasant news. It's like she felt my discontent through the wires of the telephone.

I told her about my day. I told her about Sue and Adelphi, Looting Larry and Robbing Randy, Phil and Jerry. I told her how I felt like I couldn't deal with it and that maybe it wasn't for me. There was quiet on the phone for a moment; one of those kinds of quiet where you know you're not supposed to speak because the other person is going to come up with something spectacularly brilliant. You just sort of wait it out, patiently, until they gather their thoughts. Then, with a deep breath, she said, "Obstacles." She paused. "These things are all obstacles. We've been through this before, remember? I told you that it wasn't going to be easy. People aren't going to be easy on you and if you expect them to, if you expect them to make things easy on you, then you're setting yourself up for a great big fall. You remember any of that?"

"Yeah, I do. I really do. It's just that -"

"It's just nothing! You take a deep breath and you get the hell back on the horse. That's it! Don't use these people as an excuse to quit. They've got their own lives to worry about. Right now, they're not thinking about you. Do you think they are? Do you think they're all gathered around, drinking goddamn cocktails, thinking and talking about you?"

"No."

"No, they're not, so cut all this crap out and start getting ready for tomorrow. Eat a little something, take a nice hot shower and relax a little before bed. Ok?"

"Ok. You're right." She was right. I'm always worried about what someone else thinks or how some other person perceives me. It's a real problem of mine. I'm also always using people and things as excuses to get out of doing certain tasks or to not deal with particular situations. Like, I'll say, 'I can't possibly go to school because the teacher hates me and picks on me.' That's the kind of thing I'll say to get out of going to class. Pretty lame, I know. It's a bad - very bad - habit and I really have to work on that. It's on a list of things I'm trying to change.

After we hung up, I took a nice, hot shower. It, incidentally, was one of the best showers I've ever taken. I felt the weight of the miserable day cascade down my body, along with the steaming droplets of water, down into the drain.

I literally stood under the shower head for an hour, just letting the water glide down my neck and back.

Afterwards, as I lay in my bed, waiting for the sandman to make his move, I realized that my father hadn't asked me how my first day of night classes went. I mean, this wasn't breaking news. As I already explained, he's not the type of guy who asks you if you were doing okay or anything. I told you, it's just not his way. I don't think a bunch of people ever asked him how in the hell he was doing when he was growing up. You kind of have to be operantly conditioned into doing a thing like that. What I mean is, people don't just fly out the ol' womb possessing common courtesy. Still, I wondered if he even cared. I mean, you would think a dad would want to know how his kid's day went. I might be crazy, but I think that's something a billion other dads would ask their sons.

I also wondered about Judith. I know she loved me and all - at least I think she did; but, I wasn't sure if she *loved* me. She was kind of abrasive over the phone, which is exactly what I needed; however, there was something missing. I can't really describe the feeling, you just have to know her to get what I'm saying. Something just wasn't right.

I lay there on my bed, looking up at the ceiling, surrounded by the quiet of the darkness - except for the street lamps below that gently cast a glimmer of light into the room - wondering about all of those things, then, out of nowhere, the sandman came in with an uppercut and knocked me out like a Mike Tyson blow to the temple.

FOUR

The next day I decided that I was going back to school. The thing is, I had a dream - more like a nightmare - that I was washing windshields at the intersection of 138th Street and Willis Avenue. That's a pretty crappy neighborhood in the South Bronx. I was washing these windshields with my cracked bucket filled with soap and water, and people were either flipping me nickels and dimes or flipping me the bird. I woke up from the dream in this tremendous puddle of sweat and, to be honest, that pretty much helped me figure out what I needed to do.

I figured I'd go a little early to get a good look around the campus while it was still daylight, this way there'd be no repeat of last night's catastrophe. This time, after getting a lay of the land, I'd know where the hell I was going. Like I told you before, City College has a beautiful campus with trees and grass and birds and junk like that. I got a buzz out of that about City College; you could just sit down on the benches and just be. Nobody would bother you for anything. It was peaceful. I could just sit there for hours thinking about things without a single care in the world.

When I got to the front entrance, I sort of looked around for ol' Jerry and his moron sidekick, Phil, because I was ready with my ID this time. Funny thing, it was in my bookbag the entire time, right there between the wrapper of the Reese's Peanut Butter Cups and the half empty bag of Cheese Doodles, the crunchy kind. I didn't see them, though - the dynamic duo, Jerry and Phil. They probably only worked the night shift or something. Who cares?

I started walking around, getting a feel for the place and enjoying the serenity when this goddess walked up to me. She had long, wavy, auburn colored hair and just about the best complexion I have ever seen. It was golden brown, my personal favorite. Maybe she was going to ask me if it'd be alright to have sex right then and there. I mean, I've seen it go down just like that a thousand times on that porn VHS video tape that my father hides on the top of his bedroom closet; the one he thinks I don't know about. I've literally watched that thing a thousand times. The same tape, I swear.

"Excuse me." Immediately, with those two words, the allure was gone. The thing is, she had one of those sonorously coarse voices; the kind of voice that makes you wonder whether or not she used to play football in high school and go by the name of Steve. "Is the lecture on the analysis of women represented in literature at the Great Hall? Is it there and are we late for that or what? Do you know?" I guess she thought I was there to attend that lecture or something, but, man, that voice. I couldn't get past it.

She was cute, she really was. If she'd only kept her mouth shut I'd have been able to maintain this terrific erection I had going on just looking at her magnificent body; she was a real smoke show otherwise. I wanted to fornicate with her pretty badly. Not so much with her, to be honest; just kind of in general. As I mentioned earlier, things weren't doing so hot with Judith and I was like a dog in heat for anything that had a pulse. Please don't think less of me. It's really not my fault. It's kind of a natural phenomenon. No, really, it is! It's considered like a basic human need along with water and food and all; that's a well documented fact.

Anyway, I replied, "No, I don't know." I put on this super sexy, mysterious voice when I said it. The kind of voice that entices women. The kind of voice that makes them melt like hot candle wax. The kind of voice that makes them submit to me and grant my every wish and desire. The kind of voice that turns them into silly puddy right before the eyes. The kind of voice that makes them want to rip off their clothes and have hot, nasty, harmful sex.

"Oh." She replied, shrugging her shoulders. She then turned around, walked away and just like that, she was gone. There went that.

I went on looking around, trying to appear like a goddamn regular; whatever that might have looked like. The more I walked around, the more I fell in love with the place. There were people laying around on this grassy hill that went down about twenty feet, leading to an underground passage. The passages, incidentally, were connected to all of the buildings on campus; so, people could run to them in case of a nuclear explosion or some crazy thing like that. Humankind would survive the apocalypse and be repopulated with City College students. It was pretty cool. Anyway, I saw some students and professors just walking and talking like goddamn buddies. I wasn't used to that. I mean, in high school, kids would usually run and hide from the teachers if they spotted them coming down the hallway, not going for strolls with them. I have to tell you, though, I liked it. I really did. One other thing that was pretty cool, every time I passed someone, they smiled at me. At first, when this guy passed and smiled, I was all set to beat the living crap out of him. I thought he was being some kind of fruity wise guy. That is until I realized it wasn't just him, it was everyone; it began to feel really good. It was like they were accepting me into their little circle, their little family.

I even had a great time at class that night. I actually paid attention and learned a lot. Also, Sweet Sue didn't seem so obnoxious, Adelphi chose a pretty decent name (Adorable Adelphi), and Looting Larry and Robbing Randy weren't there. As a matter of fact they never came back. They were probably looting and robbing, who knows. Phil and Jerry even gave me a wave and a nod as I left the campus - once I flashed my ID, that is, which I was wearing around my neck with an ID holder that read 'City College' all over it. I got it at the crazy school book store to kind of get into the school spirit. Things were okay that day. They really were.

On the way home from class that night, I thought about my future. I thought about who I was (nobody) and what I could become. I thought about how free everyone seemed to be on campus; how they seemed to know who they were and what they stood for. I also thought about how beautiful the campus was. I thought about those trees, the grass, the birds. I liked it. I really did. I began to feel this kind of strange sensation in the middle of my chest; it's kind of hard to describe, but if you absolutely made me try to explain the feeling, I'd say it was like something inside, deep down inside, was sort of compelling me to move forward. Like a weird gravitational push to want more, to do more, be more. I don't know, that's the best way to describe it. Anyway, that's what I did. I went forward, full steam ahead. I went to class every single day and burned the midnight oil at night; I completed all the assignments, passed all the quizzes and even participated in class. I didn't recognize myself; I was a new me.

FIVE

It was about two months later when my results for the equivalency test came in the mail. It was on a slightly overcast and unusually chilly Saturday morning in late August when I pulled out the large white envelope from the mailbox. I must say, I cannot recall ever being so nervous in my entire life. It was really stressing me out. I don't remember doing so well on the test. As a matter of fact, I was feeling pretty crappy that day. I was beginning to have these kind of heated arguments with Judith and we had one that day - the day of the test. The thing is, she had the nerve to say she was going out with one of her friends while I was taking my test, which absolutely made me lose my marbles. I mean, wasn't she supposed to be home, biting her nails, wearing out the carpet pacing back and forth worrying about me? Wasn't she supposed to be waiting for me by the door until I came back home, anxiously awaiting news of how I think I had done? Wasn't she supposed to have a nice meal of steak with onions and peppers and a side of goddamn garlic mashed potatoes waiting for me on the table to replenish the energy and hard work I had expended and perhaps rub my stupid temples after that arduous exam? Sure she was. I've seen it an endless amount of times in shows and movies. I've read it an infinite amount of times in the best written books and magazines. Anyway, so I didn't think I did all that well on the test. When I opened the crazy envelope, there was a letter and a diploma attached to it. I had passed the test after all.

It was the letter, not so much the diploma, which was what really caught my attention. Most of it went on about how thrilled they were about me passing and all; but, it was the end of the correspondence that really floated my boat. The letter invited me to register to be a full time student at City College. It was sort of a bonus or something. I think I must have fainted because, let me tell you, I never imagined that I would ever get the chance to go to college. I just figured I'd get my GED and go to work in a factory, making various dildonic devices or some insanity like that; but, they were actually inviting me to go register with them. Well, that's exactly what I did, that's what I decided to do. I was going to register for classes at City (as the regulars dubbed it).

I began, at that moment, to see a light at the end of the miserable tunnel. I could see myself walking around the college campus with a damn college sweater, shooting the shit with my good ol' psychology professor discussing the meaning of all things and then swinging over to the Student Life Building and volunteering for some tree hugging social club. I saw it as clear as day and I was ready, or so I thought, to make the plunge. Move over Socrates and Aristotle, step aside Einstein and Newton; Justin Christianson was going to college.

My first time at registration was not the most enjoyable experience in my life. Back then, City College had it set up where you'd have to stand on line for every subject you wanted. There were English lines to sign up for English classes, biology lines for biology classes, and so on. All of these lines were about five miles long, so you never really got to register for the classes that you wanted; by the time you got to the front of each line, the class was full and closed out. I thought that was pretty stupid.

Boy, I'll tell you, if I ran the world it would most certainly be a much different place. It really would. People would be a lot happier and everyone would praise me because I'd change a bunch of things; the first thing being those insane registration lines. The entire student body would carry me on their goddamn shoulders throughout the campus and shout my name for all to hear, I promise you that much. I'd be a regular hero.

While waiting on one of those cheese lines, I began to notice how lonely I was. I didn't know one stupid person; and the stink of it is, everyone else knew each other. It felt like I missed some kind of pre-registration party or some crap like that. It's like they all got together before registration, ate some hors d'oeuvres, and had long and intricate discussions about the current civil war in Russia, while the caterers walked around handing out pigs in a blanket and cheese puffs or some insane thing like that. My invitation must have gotten lost in the mail. That's probably what happened.

As I was standing there, I honed in on a couple of interlocutors having an intense conversation, two real studious looking types; the sort that wore those colorful rugby shirts with the pressed khaki pants and brown loafers and threw their heads back while they snickered at some joke the professor said that probably was the furthest thing from being even remotely funny. It was like the unofficial uniform of the day for that classification of people. Bookworm types.

"Hey, Chad, are you totally taking Faducci's philo class? He's aces, dude." Philo, as it happens, is what you called philosophy because there's absolutely no time to waste articulating a word to its completion in the collegiate world.

"Dude, yea, I totally got in because I know a dude."

"Dude, righteous! We can, like, totally share notes!"

"Dude!"

"Dude!"

As mind numbing as that conversation was, it played a significant factor in my thinking. I thought, man, these guys were really super into school. It was kind of a nice thing. I actually wanted to be a part of that insanely droll dialogue, if you can believe that. I wanted to interject and say, "Dudes, that's really totally super cool. Who'd you say that far out, rockin' philo professor was, again? I totally wanna reg for his class and like totally wanna discuss Plato's Allegory of the Cave all night long." I didn't though. I didn't partake in the meeting of the minds. Instead, I just kept to myself and registered for all my classes, which, thank the registration gods, I was able to get, in spite of the long lines.

That's pretty much how it was for the first couple of months. I was sort of a loner; I don't make friends too well, if you want to know the truth. The thing is, I'm not sociable. I'm sort of a misanthrope, to be honest. That, plus the fact that I'm very picky in that area. Like I explained before, I wasn't used to dealing with people and they weren't exactly giving me a reason to fall madly in love with them and go running and rolling down a hill into a field of daisies together. I guess that's another thing I'd like to change about myself. It's another thing to throw on that good old list of mine, so I can be a more enticing individual.

I'd like to be one of those guys that shows up at a gathering with my hair slicked back drenched with fancy grease and intelligently parted to the side, with a classic, black bow tie and pressed, black, Armani suit - like the Great goddamn Gatsby. I'd glide into the room and immediately have around ten girls hanging on every word that spills out of my miserable mouth. They'd giggle at anything remotely humorous I would say and look pensive and nod like crazy when I philosophized about the deeper issues of life. A real worldly kind of fella. That'd be me. I'm honestly going to work on that. I really am.

What I did was, instead of hanging out with friends I didn't have, I'd sit on one of the benches on campus and write letters to one of my elder cousins on my father's side of the ol' family, Juliana Christianson. Juliana was a student at Georgetown University. That's a pretty prominent woop-de-doo college down in Washington, DC. She had been in college for two years already and I figured I could get some advice from her. I'd write letters explaining how lonely I was feeling and how I really didn't know anyone. I'm pretty good at writing. I can really express what's going on inside my certifiable brain with the old pen and paper. I mean, I'm no honors English student or anything insane like that; what I mean is, I'm not too sharp with grammar and syntax and all that jazz, but I can really pour it on with ideas. I'm pretty good at just spilling my guts all over the place in black and white is what I'm trying to tell you. In my humble opinion, I think people ought to be able to just write down what they feel and hand it to their dialogist instead of having to confront them verbally. A lot more would be accomplished, that I'm sure of. Think of all the things you could say to a person if you didn't have to actually sit there and have them looking right at you as you speak. One thing is for certain, you would never have to worry about that enormous piece of spinach between your teeth as you're speaking, that's simply a serious conversation ender. Just consider it, that's all I'm asking.

Anyway, Juliana and I were really close as kids. You can basically say that we grew up more like brother and sister, rather than cousins. Every weekend, when my family got together at my grandmother's old apartment up around 184th Street and the Grand Concourse in the Bronx, we would run straight to the bedroom and begin playing some kind of make-believe game;

we would pretend to be superheroes or some other kind of adventure filled game and we'd do this for hours on end. The fun lasted for about twelve years, until ol' Juliana reached her pubescent years; then, without any kind of warning whatsoever, she became conservative, uptight, unpredictable, intolerable - in short, she was becoming a young woman; which, I hadn't understood in the least. I mean, as far as I knew, she was just being a jerk. I started to hate her, I really did. She never wanted to play anymore. She just wanted to do homework and read books. That's it. How boring. At least that's what I thought then. What did I know? They say boys are ten years younger in the mind as opposed to their chronological age; and, conversely, girls - so the saying goes on - are ten years older in the mind. I don't exactly remember where I heard that, but it's a real thing. Just ask anyone; they'll tell you exactly what I just said.

For years, Juliana and I hadn't spoken to each other. She had gone her way - the way of the scholar - and I had gone mine - the way of the junkie. Through the family grapevine, I used to hear how well she was doing, going to Walden High School in New York City, very prestigious. She was pulling A's out of her ass. Very intelligent. I also heard that, while doing all that studying, she actually passed out a few dozen times from exhaustion. I could never understand what the big deal was. I mean, what was so important about getting A's all of the time? What was the big deal? There were times when I felt like giving her a call and asking her, "Listen, I was just wondering if you could tell me what the big deal is. The fancy school, the impeccable grades. What's the big deal?" At that time, to me, it really didn't make a whole lot of sense. That was all changing now. I was finding out what the big deal was all about. At about the time when I finally started pulling myself together, she and I connected again and, as I mentioned, had begun corresponding via letters to each other.

I pulled the most recent letter that she had written to me from my jacket pocket, unfolded it, and re-read it. I will hold off from reproducing the letter right now, though. The reason being that, at this point, it didn't bear much meaning to me as it did later on in the story, so just be patient. I'll get to that a bit later. Just don't forget to remind me about it if I don't remember. I'm pretty forgetful sometimes. I think it has something to do with this bad accident I had as a kid. When I was about four years old, my forehead kind of got split open while I was jumping on the bed like some kind of deranged monkey. I ended up with a bunch of stitches, some pretty vicious migraines from time to time, and a bad memory.

Anyhow, I folded the letter and placed it back into my jacket pocket. I pulled out my spiral notebook from my bookbag and began to write back to her when this very captivating and stunningly beautiful girl walked up to me. She was really pretty. She had long, black hair that matched her beautiful eyes of the same color. She had the whitest skin I've ever seen. Not a dead, rigor mortis looking white, but a relaxing, creamy frosting kind of white. It was fair; like untouched snow just after it falls from the sky. She wasn't exactly an Amazonian; she was about thirty-seven feet shorter than me, she was about 5'1", which was okay because her magnificently toned body made up for it. She had this adorably toned body. You could tell she worked out in the gym. She was wearing these tight, hot-pink spandex pants that looked as though she'd painted her athletic looking legs pink. Underneath her halfway zipped Nike running jacket was an electric-blue spandex shirt pushing up - and almost out of their cradles - two of the firmest set of breasts I had ever seen in my entire life. I would like to have done the horizontal mambo with her right then and there, right out in the open, on campus, for the world to witness.

You have to understand, things like that don't usually happen to me; beautiful girls walking up to me and all. I mean, I'm not taking anything away from my looks, because like I told you, I'd just as soon run naked in the woods and be with myself, like Mr. Whitman in 'Song of Myself.' I'm a real 'cat's meow.' It's just that girls don't usually come up to me, that's all. Sometimes I think, perhaps, I'm too good looking. That kind of a thing can frighten girls away. It really can. It's like they think maybe I'll reject them or something. Who knows?

She introduced herself to me. "Excuse me." Just as I imagined, just as I had wished and hoped; her voice was magical. It was the kind of voice that could make you do just about anything. Like, she could tell you to jump off a roof or something and you'd wind up taking the express elevator straight to the penthouse of some one hundred and third floor high rise building and happily plunge to your death just because her voice was so hypnotic. "You're in my English class, right? With professor Marrick? My name is Emily, by the way."

I told her I was in Marrick's class, but that I hadn't seen her before. I really hadn't. I would've remembered seeing such a magnificent specimen, such a work of art, right off the paint brush of Michelangelo.

"That's because I sit behind you. I guess you just didn't notice me." She said, with disbelief, as though I upset a balance in time and space for not noticing her. "Anyway, I wanted to know if we're supposed to write that essay, about the duality of man, at home or if we're supposed to do it in class. Do you know?"

She was talking about some crazy essay we had to write about our goddamn selves and explain how we are more than just one person, like there are different versions of ourselves depending on the situations and circumstances in our lives; some real deep, Carl Jungian stuff. We had to include every detail of all our selves and really lay it out there in terms of who we all are and why. Personally, I didn't think it was anyone's business who I was and how many people I had floating around in my head. I mean, if the professor really cared, why didn't he just call me up and ask me privately or something? The thing of it is, I don't want that kind of thing on paper for everyone to read, that's pretty incriminating material. What I mean is, if I wanted to be the goddamn President of the United States, that kind of a thing could ruin me. Just when everyone thinks it's a shoo-in, and I'm about to give my victory speech, my opponent would pull out this psychotic college essay basically laying it all out there about my dual personalities. Political suicide. No thanks.

Anyway, I responded to Emily, "I believe it's in class." I answered her in my best James Bond-ish, sexy voice; and, to really lay it on thick, I gave a good pass of my fingers through my hair for added sex appeal, my go-to move. It's a real crowd pleaser, that move - right out of the suave and debonair playbook; some real young John F. Kennedy stuff. I suggest you try it, if you have good hair, that is.

"Oh thank God. I hadn't written anything. By the way, my name is Emily, Emily Soto, but I think I already told you that, didn't I? She said in such a melodic voice.

"Yeah, you did." I giggled like a thirteen year old school girl. She was so hot that she was making me sort of shy. "Mine is Justin. Justin Christianson."

"Hi, Justin. Are you a freshman?"

"Jesus, do I look that obvious?" I asked quite concernedly. I wanted her to think I was a man of experience, not some rookie freshman. Girls prefer that. Experience. They really do. I mean, look, no one wants you fumbling around for ten hours like some kind of a goofball with their bra strap, am I right? It ruins the momentum of everything. Experience is key.

"Well, it's just that you're sitting here alone. I just figured maybe you didn't know anyone. Sort of like a freshman." She said with the most adorable smirk and shy, darting eyes that ping ponged from my face to the floor and back again.

"You're right," I said with a kind of defeated tone. "I don't know anyone." I must have looked like such a moron, sitting there alone. How lucky I was to have the most beautiful girl I had ever seen so graciously point that out to me.

"Well, now you know me." She was so beautiful. I wanted to grab her and copulate with her. I didn't, though. I don't have the nerve for that kind of thing. Instead of having sex with her, I asked her if she would like to sit down on the bench with me. Maybe I could charm her with some sensuous words. I'm quite the sweet talker. Very charming. I glided over a scooch to allow for her to snuggle into the remaining tight space left on the bench.

"Thanks. I can only stay for a bit." She said, taking a seat next to me and tossing her long, black hair - which, incidentally, smelled of strawberries and cream - to the opposite side, exposing more of that flawless face of hers. "I have to meet my husband in a few minutes."

Instantly the sound of an eighteen wheeler's brakes and tires screeching to an abrupt halt entered into my head. I felt my heart slip out of my ass and slide down my leg. Husband! I was instantly turned off. I wanted, at that point, post haste, to get the hell away from her. Who needed her anymore? She was useless now. She was no longer a tool for my sexual desires. She was married. To hell with her and her lousy husband. I couldn't fathom the use of someone who couldn't satisfy my primal needs, that's how I thought back then. I was a real tool, I know. You don't have to tell me, I already know. At that point, I had to get away fast. I heard her mumbling something in the distance, but I paid her no mind. I was busy trying to figure out how in God's name to get the hell out of there. "Do you have the time?" I finally interrupted her.

"Oh, yes," she looked at her very handsome, I must say, silver and gold Tag Heuer watch. "It's a quarter to one."

"A quarter to one?" I responded like I'd missed the last train out of Dante's Inferno. "Jesus, I totally forgot about the phone call. You see, I have to make this phone call -"

"It's okay, go ahead." She interrupted, seemingly disappointed. "I understand. I'll see you in English."

"Yeah, see you in English." I ran the hell off. I was a terrible person. Save your breath, I already know.

SEVEN

What I did, what I decided to do after wandering the campus like a lost soul, was give Judith a call. We hadn't been too tight lately, as I mentioned; we used to be real tight. That is, until I began messing the whole thing up. I mean, she didn't say it, but I could feel it. I suppose I kind of understood. I think maybe I was smothering her or something. I'm not too sure. I mean, I depended on her a lot, I really did. She helped me to get on my feet again for Christ's sake. Jude - that's what I called her sometimes - never gave up on me while I was doing all of those drugs and things. I always loved her for that. She never hung up on me when I called her at three in the morning, high on some crazy drug. She never hung up. Some other girl might have lost her mind and told me to go to hell or something. Not Jude, though. Not her. I think having to deal with me was a lot of pressure on her. It's not easy to have to deal with a strung out loser on coke and crap, I'll tell you right now. Anyway, I decided to give her a call on one of the pay phones in Shephard Hall, which was like the oldest building at City College. It's supposed to be like this major landmark or something; it was built by this guy, George Post in the early 1900s. It was one of my favorite Halls on the campus because, besides the fact that it was an awesome structure - it looked like some kind of a medieval castle right out of the days of kings, queens and knights and all that. It just made me feel like I was around during those times, when life was simpler. I'd have done great in those times, I think. I would have been somebody and made something of myself. Things seemed so structured back then. That's what I need. Structure. I'm the kind of person that requires guidance, someone to point me in the right direction, someone to tell me, step by step, how to do a particular thing. At least that's what Judith tells me. Talk to me like I'm four years old is what I always say. I'm good with that. I prefer it, actually.

Anyway, I dropped a quarter into the pay phone and dialed her number. I let the phone ring about fifty times. No answer, except for the answering machine, which instructed me to leave a brief message at the sound of the beep. I hung up the phone and, as the quarter dropped down inside the coin chamber, I stood there for a while. I almost didn't know what to do with myself. I didn't like that feeling. It was almost as if, because I didn't get to speak to her, I wasn't able to move or do anything. It's like I was catatonic or some ridiculous thing like that. That's a real thing, you know. I'm not making it up. People just up and freeze when they experience a traumatic event. They just sit there with their eyes open for days, months, years. I wouldn't make a thing like that up. I mean, I may embellish a little from time to time, but I wouldn't just outright lie about a thing like that.

After about a couple of centuries, standing there like a crazy mime, I decided to go to the student cafeteria. When I got there, the place was pretty packed. Some people were eating, some were playing board games, and some were just talking. I found an empty seat way the hell across the place, which was ideal for a person with absolutely no social skills such as yours truly. On my way over, someone grabbed a hold of my arm. It turned out to be one of my old friends from high school, Marvin. He was sitting with two fairly good looking girls, which was funny because he was far from even remotely decent looking. He was about five foot three with thinning, unkempt, brown hair. He was wearing a white Hanes tee shirt that had yellow stains around the pit area, these ratty jeans with about a million rips in them and dilapidated sneakers with mismatched socks.

"Yo, wassup, homeboy!" He addressed me, yelling at the top of his lungs. One of the girls he was with was chewing gum like it was a damn rubber tire and the other was looking at the floor in some kind of trance.

I sort of ignored the girls and responded to Marvin. "Marv? Hey, what's going on? I didn't know you were at City." As if I were looking all over the world for him.

"Yeah, man. Yo, I wanchu ta meet muh bitches, Brittany and Pepper."

He snapped his fingers at Pepper, who was still staring at the floor in some sort of somnambulant, hypnotic state. "Hey, Pepper! Pepper, wake up, biach." He finally gave Pepper a few of these pats on the back of her head. She finally woke from her coma. "Dis is Justin. We went to Columbus High School together." The girls gave me this sort of a laborious smile. I gave it back. "Yo, sit down, man." He continued. "Whassup, kid? Tell me wass goin' on?" He seemed pretty eager to speak to me. We were semi-friends in high school. More of what one would call acquaintances. Whenever he'd see me in the hallway in high school, he'd run up to me and give me a damn kiss in front of everyone. I'm not kidding. A real kiss. On the lips. His idea was, if girls could kiss each other in greeting, so could guys. He was pretty sick. The thing of it is, the funniest part, it actually became a thing. Like, a bunch of us guys continued this madness for a whole year. We'd go around planting big old wet ones on each other's lips whenever we'd pass one another in the halls. Ridiculous. We'd have people either laughing or screaming in absolute terror at the sight of it. Come to think of it, it was pretty funny; but still sick.

I have to admit, I was kind of glad to see someone I knew at this point and time, albeit this creep, so I kind of settled in and decided to shoot the shit with him for a bit. "Nothing much." I answered. "Just walking around. You're the only person I know around here."

"Aww, that's sad, man… Why doncha introduce yourself to some girls, like I did? See, I introduced myself to these two tricks." One of the girls, Brittany, poured out in laughter at this and gave him a light, admonishing slap on his arm. With that, he grabbed the other one, Pepper, the catatonic, and started making out with her. While this was going on, Brittany chewed on her tire, gazing at her overly exaggerated painted fingernails, each nail a different neon color, bedazzled with different kinds of sparkles, much of which fell onto her jeans and down to the floor as she fidgeted with them. After about a year, he dislodged himself from Pepper and leaned over to Brittany and grabbed a hold of her lips with his lips and sucked inward like a vacuum cleaner. Pepper, at this point, returned to her apathetic torpor. The blank stare.

All of a sudden I didn't want to be there. I wanted to get far away from the three of them. I especially wanted to get away from him. Was it jealousy? Did I want to have what he had? Did I want to have mindless girls, with nothing to offer, dripping all over me? Well, yes, of course. I mean, I thought I did; but, at the sight of it right in front of me, maybe I didn't after all. Once again, I found myself in a situation where I needed to find out how to get away, far away. It was pretty hard because, after the lip locking session with Brittany, he kept talking a mile a minute about absolutely nothing. "I'm tellin' ya, man," he drolled on, "you're never gonna get anywhere in this school if ya don't network. It's all about networkin', man. Am I right, biaches?" He said to the girls, as he suddenly dove into Pepper's neck and began sucking and licking it like a kid sucks and licks his Mr. Softee ice cream while it drips down onto his knuckles. Pepper, by the by, had absolutely no reaction to this act of unmitigated, intractable, honestly quite nauseating, act of sheer lust.

On top of everything else, he used the word, 'networking.' I simply love it when a dimwit decides to use a word just because he might have heard a professor saying it once or twice (during a lecture that probably was way over his empty head anyway). Nevertheless, this was my break. "You know, that's a really good idea. I'm going to do that right now. Network. I really am." Marvin's mouth was still latched onto Pepper's neck like an algae-eating fish sucking on an aquarium tank. I got up from the table and bid farewell to the morons. "It was a pleasure meeting you, Brittany and Pepper… Marvin, take care, buddy." The girls and I exchanged phony smiles; Marvin, never dislodging himself, gave me a sort of slackly, dismissive kind of wave and then I left.

I slipped out of the cafeteria and continued to walk around aimlessly for another half hour until it was time to go to class. I felt depressed. I felt out of sorts. It felt like I didn't go with the place. I couldn't help thinking, am I really supposed to be here? I hoped like hell it would get better.

EIGHT

That night, I spoke to Jude. It was around nine when I called her. Things, at that point, were starting to decline severely, but it was on this somewhat chilly and rainy night that marked a pivotal point of our relationship. I tried to call her earlier and, if you recall, she wasn't home or didn't answer the phone to be more accurate. I guess I was kind of holding a grudge against her for that. If you want to know the truth, I think people should be home if you want to talk to them. They should either sit there all day waiting by the phone, anticipating its ring, or - at the very least - they should know when you're about to call and they should drop whatever they're doing and race home to receive it. Anyway, I was holding a grudge. "Where were you earlier?" I asked with my best grudge voice. You have to put on your best grudge voice if you want people to really know you're upset. You have to sell it; otherwise, they won't know how pissed off you are and will continue to aggravate you, endlessly.

"I was with a friend." She sensed my attitude. "Why?" She asked, seemingly very annoyed and displeased at the interrogation.

"What friend? Where?"

"Oh my God, seriously? Kathy. I was with Kathy in her house. Is there a problem with that?" She was really agitated.

"I called earlier. I really needed to talk to you. I mean, why is it that whenever I need to talk to you, you're at someone else's house?" My voice was starting to tremble a little. I was losing my cool because, to be brutally honest, I knew that I was nothing without us f I pissed her off too much, I'd lose. She didn't need me, I needed her; and I think she knew that. I think she knew that very well. I sure as hell knew it.

"First of all, I'm not always at someone else's house. Second, I don't see what the big deal is. If you have something to tell me, why don't you tell me now? I mean, what are you going to do, argue about why I wasn't home for God's sake?" She was at the beginning stages of a yell, very authoritative. Intimidating, in fact.

"What if I don't want to tell you now? What if I forgot what I was going to say?" I was rambling and, quite truthfully, being an infant about the whole thing. There was no point or logic to my argument and we both knew it, except I was too riled up to cut it out.

"I don't see the point to this conversation. I really don't, Justin. I've had a long day and I'd like to get some rest."

"You've had a long day? What exactly consists of a long day at Kathy's goddamn house? Painting nails and talking about guys you'd like to -"

CLICK.

I held onto the phone and listened to the dial tone in disbelief for a while. I had gone too far and I knew it. I deserved to be hung up on. I'd have hung up on me, too. The thing is, it was the very first time she had ever hung up on me and it was a devastatingly frightening feeling. My inability to function without her was overwhelming. It was like the world was crumbling down around me and I was helpless.

I paced around my room for a couple of hours, still in shock at having been hung up on by Judith. A million and one thoughts were racing around inside my skull and I couldn't make sense of a single one. I then decided to get the hell out of there. I had absolutely no idea where I was going to go, but I knew that I couldn't stay there. It felt as though the walls were closing in on me and I started seeing these little stars swimming around my eyes. Not a very good feeling at all. I threw on a white t-shirts and jeans, slipped on my Timberland boots, grabbed my jean jacket and headed out the door.

By the time I got outside, I figured I'd go over to Fordham Road, which is quite a bit of a hike from where I lived, where I could buy a bottle of beer. You can't get beer around my area because they're really strict about being 'of age.' Personally, I think that rule sucks. It's not like I have a car to drive through a building or anything. That twenty-one and over rule should only apply if you're driving. I'm serious. You'd think that an underaged scholar, like myself, could get completely and uncontrollably inebriated once in a while. It's a stupid law.

I headed over to Fordham Road (which was about a fifteen minute walk from where I lived), but when I got there, I didn't feel like getting drunk anymore. I don't know why. I guess I just wasn't in the mood. You have to be in the mood to drink, otherwise you'd be an alcoholic or something. Plus the long walk kind of cooled me off and relaxed my mind a little. It's a pretty good stress reliever. Walking. I highly recommend it if you're ever thinking about putting a couple of your fists into a concrete wall. Take a walk instead; it'll hurt a lot less, that much is for sure.

What I did instead was, I walked all the way back to my block and went into this huge park that was around there. It was night time, so the park was empty. I headed over to these swings and started swinging like a little kid. Boy, did I wish I was a little kid again. I wished that I could just start over. I began thinking of an age that I'd like to start over from. I think, if I had a choice - if I found a genie bottle, rubbed it and a goddamn genie popped his head out and granted me a choice of an age I could return to - it'd be fourteen; right before high school started. I'd make so many changes, I'd do so many things differently. I wouldn't have made acquaintance with the people I did or do the drugs I did. It would've been great. I would have gotten great grades and gone to a great college, like Juliana, my cousin.

Lost in thought, I began swinging higher and higher, without paying any mind to it, and, if it hadn't been for the policeman, I would have done a 360 degree loop-de-loop and bashed my skull into three million pieces. "Hey you, on the swing, this park's got a curfew. You're gonna hafta leave." He was an older policeman, around his late forties, early fifties, very overweight, and stressed out looking. He had these dark circles under his sleep deprived eyes and salt and pepper hair; that is, what little hair his balding head managed to desperately hang on to.

"I'm sorry?" I hadn't the slightest idea what he was talking about and I was still swinging. I was still sort of lost in thought.

"You will be, 'sorry', if ya jerk around with me. You understand, boy?"

"I'm not sure that I do." I said. I began to slow my swing. I really had no idea what he was talking about. I didn't know that there was a time that you had to be out of a playground. Apparently it was a high crime to be inside there after a certain time of night. It's right up there with murder and burglary. Serious stuff.

"You're a real wise ass, aren't ya? Well, I know just the thing for wise asses."

At that moment, just as he was approaching me with a nightstick, someone started screaming over his police radio; something about gunshots and a store being robbed. The cop gave me this 'you got away this time' look and ran off to save the day.

I'm pretty sure you could try to imagine how fast I took off, but I don't think you could. The thing is, I didn't want the fat son of a bitch to change his mind and turn back for me, so I ran all the way home. At least, I tried to. About half way back to my building, I wanted to vomit. I couldn't catch my breath and I felt like throwing up all over the place. It's not too often I get to display my keen Jesse Owens style running skills, so I figured I'd stop and regurgitate for a few minutes.

NINE

Things were pretty slow between that night, with the cop, and Christmas time. Emily, the married girl I told you about in school, and I - believe it or not - were getting to be pretty good friends. Don't ask me how, it just happened. We had the same English class, so it was kind of hard to avoid her. She was pretty persistent, too. She'd always strike up these conversations about nothing at all. She kind of softened me up, the way an invading army softens up an impenetrable structure with an endless barrage of artillery fire. We helped each other pass the first semester. I got two A's and three B's and wound up with a 3.5 grade point average, which was pretty good. I guess. It's like the lower end of an A overall. They've got this crazy chart that tells you how to convert letter grades like A, B, C to numbered grades. It's a whole thing, don't ask me to explain. You're just going to have to look it up yourself; that is, if you even give a rat's ass.

Anyway, Christmas weekend came around and since my father was a manager of a retail store, he had to work. I didn't have enough money to go see my mom in Georgia (which I did from time to time by either hopping on a Greyhound bus or the Amtrak train, even though - had I not made the effort of going to see her - she would probably forget who I was); Judith was, unfortunately for me, spending time with her family (yes, miraculously we were still together); so, I spent the weekend in Staten Island with my uncle and aunt, Felix and Gloria Christianson, and their children, my cousins, Felix Jr., Anthony, and the baby, Barbara. They had a Christmas party in which my aunt Gloria's entire side of the family and close friends showed; which meant that I would have to spend the whole evening running away from Bertha, one of the friends of the family, who was a few pounds shy of being Mount Everest. Bertha was quite heavy. She had a huge crush on me, as well as every other human male that lives and breathes. She, for years - whenever I would visit, would chase me around the neighborhood trying to plant her kisser all over me. She even, once or twice, tried fondling my unmentionables - on the rare occasion she'd actually manage to corner and capture me. For the life of me, though, I don't know why I never told her to let me alone. Maybe it was because (in a subconscious way) I actually liked the attention. I liked the fact that someone was paying attention to me - something I was lacking with Jude. I found myself, even outside of the Bertha situation, seeking the attention of anyone that would give it. I'd do various things to get people's attention and I'd always watch to see who may be looking at me. Emily says I'm a narcissistic and neurotic person. She says if I'm not careful, I could become some kind of sociopath like those crazy serial killers you read about. If you ask me, I think that's a little overboard, but I do admit that it's sort of nuts that I go around desiring the attention of crazy Bertha and others. That much is for certain. I have to work on that.

Anyway, back to what I was telling you. The best part of the party was that this was family, which meant that I didn't need any damn ID to get my whistle wet with a tall glass of rum and Coke. At first, my Uncle Felix had a bit of difficulty accepting this. As the rum disgorged from the bottle and into the very tall glass, my uncle gazed at me with a wolf-like stare and said, "I know you're pouring that drink for me, right, Justin?"

I decided to act suave, cool about the thing. Remaining calm in these types of situations is key. You can't panic or react in any sort of way that would show weakness. It's how our entire species - the stinking human race - got to the top of the ol' food chain. Early man didn't lose his shit in times like this, so I had to act the part. "This drink, brother of my dear father, is for a man. This is a man's drink."

I thought the humor would knock him off his socks and lighten up the surly look on his mug, but nothing doing. With the same, mirthless countenance he said, "Drinking age is exactly twenty-one, my young child. Give it here." He held out his paw with the intentions of purloining my precious drink.

I had to stay strong. I had to somehow cajole him, to persuade him, with my charming ways to let me have that drink. The smell of the rum, which was coconut flavored, exuded from the cup and undulated in and around my nostrils. I couldn't give up now. "Come on, tell me honestly, Unc, who the hell in this house is exactly twenty-one? I mean, you're not exactly twenty-one, you're like a hundred years old and you're drinking!"

After a brief moment of silence, along with an expressionless look on his face, during which time I spent holding my breath in anticipation of his response, he cracked a smile, which led to a jovial chuckle. Hallelujah! Bingo! My corny logic and charisma knocked him to the floor and, with that, he granted the libation to me; along with the one after that and the next one after that. I got plastered. Let me tell you, I got so wasted that I even gave Bertha a couple of once-overs, I really did. I started winking at her and blowing her kisses. I began working out in my mind where I could possibly take her and relieve my sexual frustrations, so to speak. The thing is, I couldn't, for the life of me, get an erection. I sort of like to have an erection before I ask a girl to do the deed with me. It's superstition or something. It's like those signs you see on the highway that tell the trucks to test their brakes before going down a vicious hill. You wouldn't want to wait until you're in a hundred mile an hour freefall to find out your equipment isn't working. You know?

Instead of doing that, instead of throwing a lay at good ol' Bertha, I shot a couple of games of pool with my cousin, Felix. He had a pool table downstairs in his basement. They lived in a private house with a pretty cool basement. It had all kinds of crazy things like the pool table, darts, a huge movie sized television and a Nintendo gaming system with that new Super Mario Brothers game. Pretty sick, I have to admit.

We played pool and had about ten drinks a piece. We started reminiscing our younger years and talking about girls and all kinds of other things. I liked that. I liked talking to him like that. It really felt comfortable, you know? I could've stayed down there forever, just shooting pool, drinking and talking. It's just too bad stuff like that has to end. Things, no matter how much you like them, always go away. Then you're supposed to act like everything's okay when they're gone. I don't mind telling you, that's something I have a great deal of trouble with. If it were up to me, I'd stay down there playing pool and drinking until I keeled over and dropped dead. I'd be perfectly fine with that. Things don't ever work out that way, though. They never do.

Anyway, we were about to begin our sixth game of pool when I had the incredible urge to ask him about his sex life. It fascinates me to hear people tell me things like that. It's like an obsession of mine. It's pretty bad. "Hey, listen." I said while racking up the balls. "You ever did the wild thing?"

That cracked him up. I asked him what the hell was so damn funny. He held up his 'wait a second' finger, took a sip of his hundredth glass of rum and Coke and said, "Wild thing? If that's what I think it is, you have got to get up on the new phrases, my man." He took his pool stick, struck the cue ball for the first shot, which in turn broke up the newly racked set of balls and got three of them in. While studying the aftermath on the pool table, he took another sip of his drink. Without looking up, he enlightened my substandard vernacular. "What you mean to say is, make love. You're a barbarian, cuz; you gotta grow up. You can't be saying crude shit like 'wild thing.' Women are beautiful creatures and need to be spoken about with respect and treated as such. You feel me?" He was a real ladies man. That's no bullshit. This guy pulled in ten girls in one month at one point. That's no exaggeration, he had the Polaroids to prove it. A regular guru on the conquering of the opposite sex.

"Alright, alright, well have you or not? Jeez!" I retorted. I was a little embarrassed because I was dealing with a professional.

"No, no, no. You have to say it. Have I what?" He was being obnoxious. It was like an agonizing lecture about the goddamn birds and bees from an adult. Just awful. He wanted to hear me say make love.

"Oh come on, Felix. Just answer the damn question, will you?"

"Sorry, if I don't know what you're asking me, I can't possibly answer you."

"Fine," I submitted, "have you made wild thing love?"

Felix began convulsing. He was laughing so hard, his drink practically ejaculated out of his mouth and nostrils and spilled all over the place. After about an hour and a half, he managed to bring himself under control. "Oh man, I haven't laughed that good in weeks. Thanks, man." He added some surplus chuckles, took a shot on the pool table - got two more balls in - and then honored me with an answer. "Sure I have made love. With Ronnie. We make love all the time, if you must know. As a matter of fact, I'm thinking about marrying her. I really love her, cuz."

I lost my mind at that point. It didn't compute. As I said, this guy was a regular lady killer. I couldn't fathom the thought of him settling down and getting married for Christ's sake. "Marrying her?" I was practically screaming. "What in the hell are you talking about?!"

"I just told you, I love her. That's why we make love, because we are in love with each other." He said, going around to the other end of the table to line up his next shot.

I absolutely didn't understand this. I mean, it's one thing to make love or whatever the hell you call it, but to get married? I started raising my voice even louder. "What are you thinking? Just because you banged this chick doesn't mean you run out and put a ring on it. It's just sex. That's all. The ultimate goal is to get sex, nothing else! It's nothing more and nothing less! It certainly does not mean that you get married and throw your entire life away! Don't you watch porno? Jeez-us!" My voice was really shaking by this point. I was really flustered.

He shook his head at me to exhibit his extreme disappointment and displeasure. Leaning into the table for a shot, he struck the cue ball and got two more balls in and then said, "Honestly, Justin, you need to grow up. You are so immature. So juvenile. The ultimate goal is absolutely not to get sex. The ultimate goal is to find someone who makes you happy. Someone who, when you wake up in the morning and go to sleep at night, you think about and smile. You can't be a kid forever, cuz. You really can't." He gave me this sort of 'get serious' look as he took a huge gulp of his drink. He sized up the last ball, leaned over, locked in on his target and took the shot; eight ball, corner pocket.

We, Felix and I, had not spoken after that day for several weeks. We didn't have a fight or anything crazy like that. We just kind of chose not to speak to each other after I left his house. I think that it was mostly my fault. I'm not very good at taking constructive criticism from people. I'm really not. I think it has something to do with my low self esteem. It's pretty damn low if you want to know the truth. I mean, I've only been conversing with you for just a short amount of time and I'm pretty damn sure you're thinking the same thing about me.

I knew he was right, just like I knew Judith was right. I was immature and I had to grow up. It's just that I couldn't make that connection in my head. I wanted to, I just didn't know how. Not exactly. Sometimes, in your mind, you know a thing, but for some God only knows reason, by the time thought transforms to action, it all goes to hell.

Anyway, I decided to call my mom, which was a very big deal. I don't know what it is, I just have something against picking up the phone and giving somebody the ol' buzz. First of all, you can't trust anyone over the phone. You can't. People can make faces at you or stick their middle finger up at you and you wouldn't even know it. You'd just continue to talk as if the person wasn't giving you the business on the other end and I'll be damned if I let some jackass make a complete fool out of me.

It was also a big deal - me calling my mother - because, as I said before, we don't talk that much, unless I kind of go out of my way to reach out to her. Don't get me wrong, it's not that she doesn't want to talk to me, I'm sure she does. It's just that, you know how it is, when people move far away it's harder to keep regular contact. Plus, sometimes I'm still mad at her for leaving, although other times I'm over it. I'm not sure how I feel, so I choose to be sort of aloof about the whole thing. I suppose today I was in a more placable state of mind.

"Hey mom, it's me, Justin."

"Hey! How's everything?" She sounded pretty happy to hear from me.

"Great, I finished school for the term and I've got a whole month off. We got the whole month of January off for crazy winter break."

"Oh wow, so how did you do in your classes?"

"How does two A's and three B's sound?"

"Alright, hey! That's great, keep up the good work!" There was a genuine sound of happiness in her voice that began to ease my spirits.

"I will. How's everything down in your parts?" I responded.

"Everything is fine down here. Anything is better than New York. When are you coming down?" She always asked me when I was coming down, but only when I'd call her. I mean, if she really wanted me to visit her, you'd think she'd pick up the phone once in a while and ask me to go. I have to admit, though, when I did go down to see her, it was sort of nice. She lives in this suburb of Georgia called Alpharetta and it's a pretty decent area. It's got lots of places to eat and some real nice parks to just relax in. More than just the neighborhood, there are times when I'm with her, that I feel like a little kid again. It's like I regress to an earlier stage of my life where I feel as though I'm safe and protected. It's pretty comforting to be honest.

"Soon." I always said that. Even though months and months could go by without me going down there.

"Maybe Jude could come along, too." She, my mom, was absolutely in love with Judith. My mom says that Jude and her are alike. In many ways, I must agree. The both of them can make anyone go out of their mind. They can. You never know what either of them are really thinking. I mean, they say one thing, but they're really thinking another. They won't ever tell you what they're thinking either; don't ever believe that they'd ever do that because they won't. You have to goddamn play charades to find out what's going on in their brains and if you don't guess right, you have to jump out of a window or something because they'll put you through the ultimate guilt trip.

"I'll talk to her and see what she says." I didn't mention that Jude and I were in a bad place. That would've taken way too much time and effort and I just didn't have it in me to get into all of it.

"I hope she can come, I'd really like to see her. Do you think she'll come over?"

"I'll see. I'll ask her. I really will." I was being evasive. I had so much I wanted to share, to get off the ol' chest; I just couldn't do it. It was as if some kind of a portcullis, those huge castle entrance doors, was slammed shut inside of my chest that prevented me from letting it come out, which was extremely disconcerting because it was the whole entire reason for me picking up the phone and calling my mother in the first place. I wanted nothing more than to be able to spill my beans to her and, in turn, for her to comfort me and tell me everything was going to be better. For the love of God, though, I couldn't do it and I don't know why. Maybe it had something to do with her hightailing it out of there when I was at such a young age. I think I just don't really trust her all that much. Like, there's just something inside that feels as though maybe, if I entrust her with my deepest, darkest thoughts, she'll jettison out of my life again. I don't want to waste all that time and effort telling her my goddamn beeswax only to have her exit stage left, you know?

"Ok, well keep up the good work and call me again soon. And don't forget to ask Jude if she'll come down with you to see me!" She said.

"Ok, mom, I won't forget. I'll talk to you soon."

I didn't get around to asking Judith because she and I were too busy fighting all of the time. The funny thing is, we never really argued about anything of importance. It always began with me wanting to talk with her or be with her, to tell her about all the things that were weighing heavily on my mind; but, it would end up with us wanting to be far away from each other. There were times when I'd sit in my room, with the phone in my hand, thinking of all the things I'd say to her. I'd express to her all of my doubts and fears and concerns and wishes. Sometimes I'd put the phone back onto the hook, fearing that we'd just get into another fight. Today, though, I decided to call her. I picked up the phone and dialed her number.

"Hello?" Her sweet voice flowed through my receiver like the melodic and harmonious sounds of Suite for Cello Solo No. 1 in G Major by Johann Sebastian Bach. I love that stuff. Classical music. I listen to it when I'm doing my schoolwork or when I'm feeling anxiety. It really relaxes my mind. You should try it sometime; I highly recommend it.

"Hey, it's me."

All of a sudden her voice flatlined like a heart monitor connected to a dearly departed loved one. It became dry and monotone. "Hey." She said.

I always wondered whether she felt the same way as I did. I mean, I wondered if she thought of me a thousand times. I wondered if she traced my name in the air until her arm ached. I wondered if she cared about me at all anymore. I never asked her, though. I never spoke to her about anything that concerned the way she felt about anything. It was just mostly about what was concerning me. I wanted to talk about us, so that we could fix things somehow. I just didn't. I left things alone to rot like meat that has been forsaken in a young bachelor's refrigerator.

"I called to say what's up." My tone now matched hers. It was bleak and hopeless, void of any feelings whatsoever.

"Nothing's up." She answered with the voice of death.

Alright, then, I'll let you go."

"Bye."

That was a truly meaningful and illuminating conversation. Full of love and passion. I was livid and decided to call back and make an issue out of that phone call. It seemed like such a good idea at the moment. What could go wrong?

"Hello?" There was that sweet, loving tone again, as if we hadn't just had the most miserable conversation in the entire universe. She clearly had no idea it was me calling again.

"Why did you hang up like that?"

"Oh, Lord." The dreary voice of disgust returned. "I had nothing to say to you."

"Why not?" My voice was shaking now. "Why don't you have anything to say to me?"

"I don't know, I just don't."

"Maybe you're telling everything to your secret boyfriend."

CLICK.

This was all too familiar. All of a sudden I felt like doing something very bad to my body. Whenever I feel miserable, I like to do bad things (drink, smoke, whatever). Being that I was too damn lazy to go all the way to Fordham Road or Jerome Avenue - another hot spot for delinquent behavior - where the good stuff could be purchased, I settled for a cheap cigar. I had picked up a pack of King Edward's cigars when I was in Staten Island with my cousin. It was an extremely low quality type of cigar that could be purchased at the local neighborhood bodega for about a dollar and, in all honesty, tasted like King

Edward's soiled underpants, but I really felt like putting something unnatural into my body. To tell you the absolute truth, I even considered getting a bag of weed, marijuana. I considered it really hard.

I decided, though, to settle for his royal highness, King Edward. I smoked it for a couple of minutes while I thought of Jude. If there were such a thing as a 'mental relationship,' we'd be the happiest couple in the world. We really would. What I mean by that is, in my mind, I'd imagine us walking hand in hand in the springtime, just a happy-go-lucky couple, doing all the things that people in love do. We'd just lose ourselves in a field of plush, green grass and wildflowers, eating snacks out of one of those wicker picnic baskets filled with sandwiches, apple pie and all other kinds of crap. No one around. Very peaceful. We'd give each other a couple of kisses now and then; I'd pick some of the wildflowers for her and she'd put one of them in her hair. Then we'd make love right there on the pillowy soft grass, the whole romantic bit. I just couldn't figure out what was going on with us; although, I had a pretty good idea it was me. Deep down in my gut, I knew I was the culprit; but, for whatever un-Godly reason, I just couldn't piece it all together; and, even if I were to piece it together and make sense of it all, I wouldn't know what to do about it. I wouldn't know how to fix it all.

ELEVEN

The month vacation went by quickly and registration time for college came again. I was glad. I don't like vacations, unless I'm doing something pretty spectacular. All I did though, during the whole month off, was stay home and watch television reruns of Bewitched, Happy Days, the Munsters and the Monkees. Although those are some damn good shows, it made me feel like a whole waste of life, so I was glad when it was time to go back to school.

I bumped into Emily at registration and we signed up for the same classes together; all with the exception of a music class. I signed up for that one alone. Emily didn't think it was such a hot idea. "Bitch," That was her name for me, 'Bitch,' because she said I acted like a queer. She was such a diva. "Why'd you do that? Why music?"

"I'm interested in classical music. I like that stuff." I really did. I could listen to Wolfgang Amadeus Mozart's Requiem or George Frideric Handel's Messiah a million times and not ever get tired of it. She, Emily, felt differently, though.

"Yeah, but it's boring. I heard it was really boring."

"You probably heard that from somebody who can't appreciate good music. That's who you probably heard it from." I said, defensively. I get defensive about stuff I like. I don't like people trashing stuff that makes me happy. It's just a thing, I can't explain it. It's like it's a part of me. It makes me who I am. I think all the things a person does, or wears, or likes, or whatever, makes up their stinking personality and you shouldn't judge it or make fun of it. Does that make any sense? I think it does, but what in the hell do I know?

"I heard the teacher is really boring." She continued. "I'm telling you, Bitch, don't do it." That was always her story; everything was boring. If she wasn't jumping out of a plane, without a parachute, with her entire body lit on fire, she was bored. In this case, though, I should have listened to her. My music professor, Constapoloducci, was an absolute drip. He absolutely ruined it for me. What he'd do, he'd sit in a far corner of the room, half dead, slumped over in his chair, and just mumble facts on whatever musical piece was playing in this sort of dreary, somber as hell voice. That really disappointed me, I can't even begin to tell you how much. I really wanted that class to be interesting. I was really looking forward to it. Sometimes I'd picture myself as a composer in those days, with the fabulous wig and fancy as hell frilly get-up just conducting away in front of the goddamn emperor of Austria, like in that movie, Amadeus - one of my all time favorite movies, in case you wanted to know. That'd be pretty awesome, to be completely honest.

What I'd do, if I didn't fall asleep all over my desk in music class, I'd sneak out the back door of the classroom and go for a beer at this Korean restaurant outside the campus. They had this area in the back of the restaurant that was all set up with tables and chairs, so that people could eat their food; a little pond with these gorgeous orange and silver koi fish swimming around; and paper lanterns that were hung up all around the joint with Korean designs on them that illuminated the eating area. It was a little cozy as hell oasis and it was pretty neat, I have to admit. I loved going there for a beer or two. Sometimes I'd sit there and just think. It really put me in this kind of meditative state. I'd just sit there with my beer and stare at those lanterns until I felt numb. Not numb in a bad way; but in this kind of relaxed, tranquil way. Like, I wasn't thinking about all of my problems at that moment. I would have recommended that you go there and see the place for yourself, but I heard that the Feds raided the establishment due to the owner trafficking humans or some madness like that. Life is a bitch; every time you start liking a place, every time you get super comfortable and start going to a place where you can just drift off and let your mind chill out, the owner ends up trafficking people and spoils everyone's good time. Some people are so selfish and don't consider others. A shame, really.

Anyway, I almost forgot, I was telling you about Emily. If you don't tap me on the shoulder and tell me that I'm rambling on, off topic, I'll end up talking your damn ear off about a thousand other things like Korean lanterns, federal crimes, or some craziness like that. Anyway, as you already know, things with Judith were really sour; I was so used to her being there for me and setting me straight that I was, at that point, completely lost without her. I was so lost that I began looking for someone, anyone, to fill that void; therefore, it was for that very reason that I began to woo my closest friend, Emily. What I'd do was, I'd write her these very charming as hell letters in class, explaining how ravishingly beautiful I thought she was, how much I liked and desired her, and how I was wondering if she'd like to go out sometime. I really didn't care about her stupid husband at that point in time, either. I know it's bad, I'm just telling you what I was feeling back then. I mean, I could lie to you. I could lie and tell you a bunch of stuff that isn't true; but, I figure I've been honest with you up until now, so it'd be pretty silly of me to start lying now.

She never reciprocated the feelings, but she never rejected me, either. I guess she didn't want to hurt my stupid feelings. A lot of females are like that. Instead of telling you to get lost, they put on these award winning performances in the hopes that you'll get the hint and leave them the hell alone. That's what she did, I think. Emily would just tell me how she'd always be there for me as my 'friend.' I hate that. The ol' let's be friends routine. They call it the friend zone. That's where I was, in the goddamn friend zone.

Let me tell you, if you're a guy, that's an extremely shitty place to be. You never get out. Ever. It's a nightmare. If a girl ever starts sharing a bunch of stuff with you that you know she'd never, ever, tell a guy she's romantically interested in, you are in this abyss of a place. Also, if you find yourself at DSW, the women's shoe store, or Forever 21 for a day of shopping, you're probably in the zone, too. Just be warned. You're only there to hold the items of clothing, or whatever, and tell her how fabulous she looks in whatever she's trying on. Afterwards, after going to about a hundred and three different stores, you'll sit down to an afternoon lunch - that you will pay for - while she drones on about some female rival at school or work, then you will carry all fifty-five shopping bags all the way to her building entrance. At this point, you'll get an air kiss to your cheek (this is a kiss that never actually touches your cheek) and the door to her building closed in your face, at which point you will hoof it all the way back home with nothing to show for your day, except a headache and no money in your pocket.

One night, though, after she and I decided to go out to a bar around 86th Street and Second Avenue, Manhattan, and throw back a few hundred rum and Cokes, I decided to make a move on her. That's exactly when you should do some crazy, ridiculous thing like hitting on your married friend, by the way; when you're pre-blackout stage drunk, that's when you should definitely make your move. There is absolutely, unequivocally, no better time to do such a thing. "Whatta ya doin afta this, muh love of muh life?" I was pretty hammered and my words were slurring. Very attractive, I know.

"I'm going home. My hubby is probably waiting for me. I'm just really worried that he's going to smell the alcohol on my breath. He's gonna kill me! He really is!" Apparently, he hated when she went out drinking. He was a health nut and thought it was a repugnant thing. He'd just as soon go for a swim in a pool filled with flesh eating piranha than have anything to do with alcohol.

Here was my opening. My big chance. "Lissen, you needa come ta muh place. Das wha you needa do. Tell yer hubby dat yer stayin at yer girlfriend's place." I was really struggling to put together these sentences. Rum and Cokes in large quantities will definitely do that to a person. It really will.

She sat pensively for a moment before answering. "That's actually not a bad idea. I really don't want him knowing I was drinking. Hang on a minute." With that, she reached into her purse and pulled out some loose change and walked over to the pay phone. After a few minutes, she came back and gave me the thumbs up signal. Apparently, she told 'hubby' that she was staying with a couple of her girlfriends for the night, so she was all mine for the rest of the evening! I was in complete and absolute joy and rapture.

Unfortunately for me and my raging hormones, we had to take the train from the bar in Manhattan all the way to the Bronx. That is the epitome of the word anticlimactic. Honestly. Within an hour, though, we were at my place, my dad's place, in my room. It was about ten o'clock at night and my dad wasn't home. This was my big moment. My heart was pounding inside my chest like a war drum summonsing a tribe to battle. The long train ride home sobered me up just enough to get my sexual juices flowing, so the stage was set for the tryst.

She, Emily, was making some sort of small talk that went completely through my right ear and out the left. I couldn't care less about what she was saying. I just wanted us to go at it, like wild animals in the jungle. As she went on about her damned husband working out at some power gym, she made herself comfortable on my bed. She removed her shoes and revealed her sumptuous toes, which were painted a tantalizing powder blue, like the color of cotton candy that you get at a carnival. I can't begin to describe to you what elation I was feeling at the sight of that, what with my love for girl's toes and all. The dress she was wearing, this hot, black number patterned with a bunch of little pink wild flowers, exposed her upper thigh as she lay on her side, with her arm propping up her head. Simply a gorgeous, flawless sight. Breathtaking.

I slithered like a python over to the bed, unbeknownst to Emily because she was still droning on about Mr. Wonderful. As she was loquaciously detailing her husband's gym routines, I began gliding two fingers up and down her leg; which seemed to have sent absolutely no signals to her brain. The synapses were definitely not firing. Little by little, my fingers traversed upward toward her thigh; however, still no reaction from her, although my male member was at full attention and my body temperature felt like it had risen about one hundred degrees Fahrenheit. Hubby's workout routines continued to spew from her mouth unto deaf ears. My phalanges ascended, now reaching that exposed upper thigh of hers; it made my heart climb into my throat, pounding against my jugular vein. My entire body felt as though it was pulsating.

As I approached the pinnacle, the bottom part of her ass, I nearly lost my consciousness. With my pointer finger, I stroked the undercarriage of her ass cheek, which was sticking out of her panties. Ever so gently, ever so slowly, I began to move her underwear to the side; all senses were lost at this point, hearing nothing but a vague murmur and seeing nothing but a sort of fuzzy haze all around me. At that moment, I moved in for the kill. Like a deep sea diver plunging into the deep ocean water, I attempted to dive into her womanhood. It was there that it all came to a bitter and tumultuous end. Grabbing hold of my wrist with a look of complete and extreme consternation, she said, "Oh my God, Justin, what the fuck are you doing?"

"I'm sorry, I thought it was ok! I mean, I thought you'd be ok with it!" I shot up and out of the bed with a clamor and stood at complete attention, the way a private in the army would if a sergeant walked into the barracks at boot camp. I think I might have saluted her, too. I'm not entirely sure.

"Why in the fuck do you think I'd be ok with you sticking your goddamn finger up my vagina?" She was practically screaming at the top of her lungs now. It was pretty scary to be honest with you.

"Just calm down, I'm sorry, I'm really sorry, just please relax!" I was pacing back and forth with no purpose out of sheer shock and absolute panic.

"Don't tell me to relax, Justin, how dare you! What were you thinking?" She was really loud and I was afraid the neighbors would hear and tell my damn father or some crazy thing like that. My neighbors had absolutely no problem dropping dimes, ratting, about the goings on in the building. Many a time, when I was much younger, I'd come home to a nice warm welcome; where my father and his belt - his weapon of choice when it came to discipline (or 'correction' as he preferred calling it) greeted me at the apartment door and subsequently beat the living crap out of me because one of the neighbors mentioned what an ass I was being earlier in the day; so, you can understand my perturbation when Emily started hollering like all hell was breaking loose.

"Emily, please stop yelling. I'm super sorry. I made a mistake, it was an accident."

"An accident? Justin, you don't accidentally slip your finger in a girl's cooch!"

"I know, I know, I'm an idiot, I'm the worst scum. I'm so sorry, Emily, please just stop screaming."

"Oh my God, you know what -" with that, she grabbed her purse and shoes and stormed out of my room and out of the apartment.

I suppose I can't blame her or anything. It's not like I came out and told her exactly what I wanted from her that night. I didn't make it abundantly clear what my intentions were. Perhaps I should've said, 'Hey, Emily, let's go over to my place because I want to do the horizontal mambo with you.' I guess I knew deep down inside that it was a pretty ridiculous thing to do. It was kind of a violation of our friendship and a pretty damn low thing to try and have sex with my married best friend. Maybe that lecture my cousin, Felix, gave me was starting to slowly sink in. He told me that I had to grow up and boy did I feel like a stupid little boy at that moment.

It took a few weeks, but after awhile, she accepted my apology (I practically begged for her forgiveness about ten thousand times and promised I'd never do such an idiotic thing again). At one point, during one of the apologies, I literally got down on my hands and knees and held onto her leg, while imploring her to absolve me. It really was a grand spectacle. Eventually, after much penance, she finally forgave me and we rekindled our friendship.

We, Emily and I, hung out quite often after that debacle. We'd grab a pizza or sit down to a nice rice and beans lunch around the school at this pretty decent Spanish restaurant. One day, though, we were walking around the campus, having a great conversation about random stuff like actors and movies and other bullshit, when she completely ruined it by bringing up her better half.

"Me and Artie are going to see a movie tonight." Artie was her ball and chain.

"Oh, really. What movie?" Like I really gave a flying crap.

"I don't know. What do you think we should see? Everything is so boring."

Why was this girl asking me what she and her stupid husband should see? If you ask me, this was part of that award winning performance I was telling you about earlier; the one where girls try to put on a grand show to get you the hell away from them instead of just coming clean and telling you to get lost. "I'm not really good at movies, I wouldn't know." I began to feel a pain in my chest. I didn't want to be around her anymore because I knew what she was up to. I knew the goal was to get away from me. What was worse, I knew I had no business feeling the way I was feeling. I had already accepted the fact that she and I were only friends; I wouldn't have made another single, solitary attempt at fornicating with her and, to be quite honest, she and I would have made a horrible couple, anyway. I mean it. She was always going out to clubs and dancing with about two hundred guys a night and then talking your goddamn ear off about her husband who, quite frankly, was getting the shitty end of the stick in that relationship. Honestly, I don't know how Artie managed to deal with it. I wouldn't have. If I were married, I'd expect my wife to be home taking care of me and spending time with me, not going out and painting the town red every goddamn night, coming home at all hours, doing God knows what. The point I'm trying to make is, if you want to galavant all over New York City, getting obliterated, you shouldn't get hitched. That's just my personal opinion.

I just found some random excuse to beat her to the punch and take off. I didn't want to spend one more fraction of a second there with her. "Listen, I've got to study for that music class now. There's a really intense exam coming up and I really have to hit the books. I'll see you later." I figured that would be the perfect excuse because, as I mentioned to you earlier, she didn't like that particular subject and, although she and I would study for all the other classes together, I knew she'd have nothing to do with my music class.

"Alright, Bitch, go study for your boring ass music class. I'll see you later." I was right. I got no argument from her. She actually couldn't have cared less, which was just fine with me.

TWELVE

Since I didn't really have to go to that class, and I just wanted to get away from Emily and get away from the confusion she caused in my noodle, what I did do was, I decided to surprise Judith and pick her up from school. I got on the Five train and, as if a miracle had occurred, I got a seat. It's pretty hard to get a seat on a train in New York City, as I mentioned to you earlier. My miracle was short lived however, when a five hundred pound guy wedged his way in between myself and the man beside me. Ridiculous.

While struggling for air, I thought some more about everything that was going on. Things weren't exactly making any kind of sense to me. Usually, whenever I'd feel like this, I could just pick up the phone and tell Jude all about it. She'd be there for me. She'd be there to make me feel better and to tell me what I needed to do. That's why I depended on her so much. Now, all of a sudden, I found myself without that crutch. She, Judith, was almost never available anymore. She either wasn't home half the time or wouldn't pick up the phone when I called. She was never there anymore to make me feel complete and whole and all together. I needed her to tell me what to do in times of peril and who I was when I got lost because, at one point in my life, she had put my broken pieces together; and now, my structure was collapsing and I had absolutely zero skills or tools to rebuild. I was regressing and no one was there to set me straight. Now I was making passes at a girl who was bored if you weren't playing Russian roulette with a goddam fully loaded gun, not to mention the fact that she was married. I was having lewd and downright heinous thoughts about girls in general that I should have been ashamed to have. Thoughts of returning to drugs and alcohol ran rampant in my mind because it, so I thought at the time, would relieve me of the burden of my reality - a reality that I did not comprehend. I was really becoming unhinged and I didn't know what to do.

This whirlwind of thoughts whipped round and round inside my head, like a hurricane blasting through a Caribbean island, destroying all in its calamitous path to the point that I almost changed my mind and got off the train, but before I knew it, I had reached 59th Street; my stop. I waited about an hour in front of Cathedral High School for Jude. I got there at about twenty after one; she didn't get out until two-thirty.

When I saw her come out of the building, I got a funny feeling in my stomach. The kind of feeling that you get when you're really nervous about something - either that, or if someone punches you in the gut with all of their might. The thing of it was, in spite of my urge to upchuck my entire stomach, I had an incredible urge to run over to her, pick her up, swing her around and kiss her a thousand times; but, when I saw the look in her eyes - the look of sheer disgust when they met mine - all those feelings of elation were shattered. Elation became animosity. Animosity became callousness. "Hey." was my salutation in this sort of expectation of glumness.

"Hey." Was her morbid reply. "I didn't know you were going to pick me up." Her eyes had the look of absolute abhorrence.

"Yeah, I didn't, either. I figured I'd surprise you and just drop by. Is that okay?"

She inhaled, held it in for a brief second, then exhaled with a slight roll of her eyes and said, "Fine. Have you been waiting long?" She asked, not really looking at me.

"No, not at all. I just got here, as a matter of fact." I didn't tell her I'd been there for an hour before she came out. Sometimes when you notice that a person lacks interest in you and your conversation - and quite possibly your entire existence - you lose the desire to get into things like that.

"Oh, that's good." She replied as dryly as a human being possibly could.

We pretty much acted like a couple of corpses for around ten blocks until we reached 68th Street. That's where I took hold of her arm firmly, but gently, and turned her toward me. "Do you think you'll ever leave me?" I was looking straight into her arrestingly captivating, perfectly shaped, almond eyes.

The wind was gently blowing her long, light brown hair into her eyes. She reached into her black leather jacket pocket and took out a flower patterned hair scrunchie, which she used to place the hairs in her face behind her head into a ponytail, exposing her now rose colored cheeks, which were a shade darker as a result of my inquiry. She had a very demure countenance now; she took her eyes away from mine and directed them to the concrete sidewalk below and said, "Why are you asking me that?"

"I don't know, it's just something I want to know. Do you think you will? Leave me?" There was a slight tremble in my voice. I don't know if she noticed, but I'm certain she wouldn't have cared.

"Look, Justin, I don't want to get into it today. I have a lot on my plate with school and my part time job and everything. I also have a really bad headache, by the way." She had gotten this job working at a pet store. Nothing spectacular, she said she just wanted to get some work experience. Apparently that's a pretty important thing in the real world. Forbes 500 companies really go bananas for people who work at local pet stores. That's the kind of employee that the wolves of Wall Street are really scouring the planet for.

What really got to me, what tore me up inside, was the fact that she clearly had no time for me. It wasn't the fact that she was busy with her new career or anything. It's the simple fact that what she was doing was taking viable time away from me. She was putting me on the back burner and I felt neglected.

I didn't reply because we would have started fighting. I didn't want to fight today. I didn't want to fight at all anymore, period. We remained silent for the rest of the walk to the train station and pretty much the entire train ride back home. All I kept thinking of, as I often do - and as I've told you ad nauseam - was how much I wished I could just start over. On that particular day, I wished I could just be in my mother's womb; just sitting in there, her stomach, and kicking back with no care, worry or responsibility in the world. The good old days. That's what I thought about the whole miserable train ride back to the Bronx, while Judith and I sat next to one another, like two rocks in a quarry. At some point, she got off the train to go to her job, which was about two stops before mine; I continued on to the Pelham Parkway stop and took the lonely walk home.

THIRTEEN

When I got home, I locked myself in my room and started reading, for the hundredth time, The Catcher in the Rye, by JD Salinger. It's about this kid, Holden Caulfield, who gets thrown out of his boarding school and spends the whole night in New York City, wondering where the ducks from Central Park go in the winter. I love that book because it reminds me that I'm not alone in feeling isolated and confused in this crazy world. I often wonder where I am in the world, like those ducks. I also love the way he, Holden - although spiritually and mentally lost in this world - seems to be in control of his feelings. Like he knows what he likes and what he despises and that, to me, is a powerful thing. I mean, no one can take that away from you, you know? No matter where he was or who he was conversing with, he was always sure of how he felt about that particular moment. I don't know, I'm no book critic or anything. I just like it, that's all. I actually wrote him a letter once, JD Salinger. He never answered me, though. I think that's because he doesn't like the human race too much. There were stories going around claiming he lives in hiding and that he wants nothing to do with the outside world. A real recluse. I don't exactly know if that's true, but I can't blame him if it is. Like I said earlier, I don't like people too hot either.

I fell asleep while reading the book and about an hour later, the phone rang. It was a female friend of mine, Selena Martin, that I had known since I was a kid. She lived about half a block away from me, but we rarely see one another nowadays. When we were kids, we used to ride our bikes all over the place and run around like little maniacs. I honestly miss that, just running around with no responsibilities, having a great time. We kind of kept in contact by way of telephone now and then, though, and today I guess she decided to give me a ring. "Hey, love! It's me, Selena! How are you?" She had this militaristic, commanding tone that made you wake up if you were in the deepest of sleep. She could have been a damn drill sergeant doing reveille in the Marine Corp, for the love of God. She'd walk right into the barracks, while the troops were fast asleep, in their tenth dream, and just rip them from their slumber. A regular authoritarian.

"Hey, Selena. What's going on?" I always got a kick out of her phone calls because she always sounded like she was in high spirits and that sort of a thing can be contagious; it winds up putting me in a good mood. She was always like that, even when we were little. Just a happy-go-lucky kind of person.

"Nothing, man. I miss you. Are you keeping well?"

"Yeah, I'm doing well. How's everything with you? School?"

"School sucks, I hate it." She went to the College of Mount Saint Vincent. It's this very cozy, quaint, Catholic College in Riverdale, New York - a very posh area - that was a page right out of that artist Noman Rockwell's work. Like, if you took a picture of Mount Saint Vincent in the winter time, after a goddamn blizzard, it would look exactly like one of his spectacular paintings. Gorgeous.

"What do you mean you hate it? Are you failing a class?" I was really concerned. She and I grew up together and I didn't enjoy hearing that she wasn't doing well.

"I don't know, I'm not sure. You can never tell about those things. One minute you think you're getting straight A's and the next minute they slap ya in the face with a D, all because you didn't know a certain thing or the other. You can never tell."

"I know what you mean. I think I'm doing okay at City. The thing is, I'll probably wind up flunking out of the place." I was taking some social science class now and I wasn't doing too great. In my opinion, it was the professor. Professor Ramses. She was a complete bore. Almost as drippy as Professor Constapoloducci, except at least she had breasts, which, incidentally, wasn't enough to get me through the class.

"I'm sure you're doing fine. You're a smart cookie." See? She's so upbeat and positive. I loved that. Then she kind of brought me down with the next question. "So… How's your girlfriend?" She knew all about Judith. She even met her once or twice; however, she never seemed to be able to address Jude by her name. She always called her my 'girlfriend.'

"She's fine, I guess." I didn't want to discuss my tribulations over the phone.

"Oh." There was silence for a while before she continued. "So, do you want to meet downstairs at our park? It's been so long, I'd like to see you if you don't mind. I mean, if I'm not disturbing you."

"You're not disturbing me at all. I'd love to meet you downstairs. I'll be down in five minutes."

I jumped out of the bed, brushed my teeth and gargled with mouthwash. You never want to have a close quarters conversation with someone if you haven't gargled. It's just downright revolting, and quite honestly extremely ill-mannered, to launch your ghastly dragon breath at anyone who is taking time out of their day to talk to you. That's not just my opinion, either. It's in some book about manners that I once read somewhere, so it's an actual rule. I then splashed on a bit of Joop, my cologne - a very alluring and sensuous fragrance, if I don't say so myself - and headed out the door. I was really looking forward to seeing Selena. For whatever unknown reason, my heart was beating just a bit more swiftly.

FOURTEEN

We decided to meet at that park I told you about before, in between our apartments. She referred to it as 'our park' because that's where we first met as little kids. We were about five or six years old when we first laid eyes on one another, back in 1980, the good old days. She was on top of the slide, her blonde hair done up in these perfectly styled pigtails, and I was climbing the steps to get to the top of the same slide. When I got to where she was, I politely said, "Excuse me, little girl."

She whipped her head around so quickly to look at me that her pigtails swirled around like helicopter blades and she said, in a very haughty and matter of fact manner, "I'm not a little girl, I'm a big girl; and another thing, don't rush me. I'll take all the time I need, thank you very much." At which point I very patiently waited for another three to five whole minutes at the top of those stairs; an eternity for a child. Ever since then, we have been friends and, let me tell you, she hasn't changed a single bit. She could lead an army into battle, that much is for certain. There's no doubt in my mind whatsoever that she could be some kind of a fifty-five star general in the army. They'd send her and her troops into battle and she'd bring all of them back home safe and sound.

Now, thirteen or so years later, I approached her at the same park. Even in the dim lighting of the setting sun, I could see Selena's sea-blue eyes focusing on me, reading me; my body language, my facial expression. They, her eyes, had the skeleton key to Everyman's being; his conscience. They compelled you, like in the Sumonyng of Everyman - this pretty intense play, written in like the 1600s by some unknown person, to face yourself in every possible aspect. In the play, the main character, Everyman, meets up with all kinds of cool characters, like Knowledge, Death, Beauty and a bunch of others. He tries to get all these guys to come along with him in the hopes that it'll make him a better person in the eyes of God. What he, Everyman, doesn't realize - what he should've known that whole time - was that he possessed all these things all along; he just didn't see it during his journey. Pretty enlightening stuff. Anyway, continuing right along with Selena, her eyes honestly penetrated my soul. I loved her eyes, I have to admit, they were really and truly like the waters on a clear day at some tropical beach; like a sky without clouds. Bewitching, honestly. "Hey babe!" She shouted. She was so full of life. Such high spirits.

"Hey, kid! How's it going?" We gave each other a kiss on the cheek and a warm embrace, then took a seat on the swings. I half consciously looked around for that police officer that I had the run-in with before, but thankfully he was nowhere in sight. He was probably devouring a few dozen powdered donuts somewhere. "You look great," I complimented. She really did. Her long, blonde hair fell gently onto her shoulders and she was wearing this very smart Arabian-sand looking pea coat with a satin, floral handkerchief around her neck. Very mature. Very high class.

"Thank you, so do you." She replied, which was complete bullshit. I had on that faded blue jean jacket, the plain, white, fruit of the loom v-neck t-shirt - untucked - with those pair of hole-ridden blue jeans that, at the bottom cuff of the jeans, tucked into my ratty pair of Timberland construction type boots that were untied with the tongue of the boot flopped downward. I thanked her for the compliment, though.

"So, are you and your girlfriend really fine or was that a load of crap? I think I know you well enough to say it was a load of crap."

It felt as though she were reading my mind. I chuckled at the thought. "I'm not too sure, if you really want to know the truth. Things are just different now, I guess. All we do is argue all the time. That's all we ever do."

"Why do you guys stay together if you argue so much?"

I replied with a long, melancholy sigh. For some reason, I couldn't answer that question. I really wasn't sure. What I mean is, there were plenty of times when I would lay in my bed, looking up at the ceiling, wondering why in God's name I was still with Judith, even when I knew it couldn't possibly work out for much longer. Still, neither Jude nor I would do a damn thing about it. We'd just stay together with a brick wall between us. It's like, I just needed to know she was there while I walked the tightrope that was my life because she was like a safety net; and, similarly, she stayed around because she knew she was the safety net and didn't want to be responsible for me plummeting to my demise, splattered all over the ground, if I were to fall. I'm no Phil Donahue, but that's my assessment of my own situation. What do I know? I could be wrong.

Besides the squeaking sound of the swings, there was complete silence for a few minutes. I kind of liked it. I liked sitting there with Selena and just swinging on the swings. I glanced at her a couple of times and I could tell she wanted to tell me something. She was making these funny faces and you could tell she was forming words in her head. "Justin?" She started.

"Yeah?"

"You know I love you. I really do. I mean, we've known each other for a very long time and I do love you very much. You know that, don't you?"

I knew that she was referring to a loving friendship that we had built over the years. I nodded to acknowledge her. I also knew that she was setting me up for a blow. You only tell someone you love them right before you hit them with a bomb, it's some kind of damn buffer. Everyone knows that.

"Listen, I know that you and your girlfriend have been together for awhile, and I know that you care for her very much. And I believe she cares for you, too; I mean, I know she cares for your well-being. I'm aware of the fact that she has essentially nursed you away from all that garbage you were putting in your system. She did what no one else seemed to be able to do." Her last words hung in the air and she sort of looked away, as if she were still unsure if she wanted to continue.

"But?" I nudged.

"But -" she was searching for the right words. "But, maybe it's time to let go." I immediately displayed a look of discontent. My eyes dove downward and my shoulders collapsed. She noticed the show of despair and disconnect, but she continued. "I know it's not something you want to hear, I know that; but, sometimes in life you have to let go of the things that were good and important and useful at one point. Sometimes you have to move on. Like, when you get a cut, you put a bandage on the wound when it's fresh, but you wouldn't keep it on forever, would you? At some point you have to take the bandage off and keep it moving. You see my point?"

I did. I did see her point. I just don't think I was ready to accept it. I wasn't ready to let go. To move on. I wasn't ready to leave the comfort, the security, of Judith. What if I fell? What if I got lost? What if I felt alone? To whom would I turn to make me feel at ease? I kept my head turned away from Selena as I answered, "Look, I don't want to talk about this anymore."

"Justin -"

"I said I don't want to talk about it. Look, you don't know what I'm going through. You don't know what it's like to be utterly alone. That's what I'll be if I leave her, you know; alone, by myself. Some friend you are." I stopped to breathe a little and also to calm myself a bit before I continued. "You know Judith is the only person I can truly count on in my life. She wouldn't be telling me some shit like this, knowing how difficult this whole thing is for me. She wouldn't." The irony of it was, Jude would absolutely, without a doubt, tell me something exactly like that. That's precisely how she spoke to me all of the time, except I wouldn't listen; just like I wasn't listening to Selena now.

She had this really affronted look on her face. "Look, maybe it was a bad idea for me to get involved."

"Yeah, maybe it was." I felt horrible and I instantly regretted saying that, but I was too stubborn and upset to give in.

"Okay. Well… Okay, then. I'm sorry to have upset you. It wasn't my intention. I was just trying to be a friend. I'll leave you be." With that, she got off of the swing, adjusted the bottom of her pea coat and walked away. I didn't stop her. I wanted to; but, even if I would have, there wouldn't be much sense in it; I was confused. The truth is, Selena was right. She was dead on. I just couldn't see it. I didn't want to see it. I didn't know how to see it. I was a mess.

FIFTEEN

For a while I was avoiding Judith. When she'd call, I would let the answering machine pick up and I think she, similarly, was doing the same to me when I called her. It was just as well, with all this confusion going on in my mind. I really needed to think things through. My world was spiraling out of control and I couldn't see a light at the end of the proverbial tunnel.

Like an angel sent from heaven, though, my cousin Felix came by to visit and told me he could stay for a few days. We had patched things up since the last time at his place and I was really glad he was coming over; because, if he hadn't, I probably would have hung myself from the rafters. He provided this kind of 'time-out' from everything.

The doorbell rang. I opened up the door and welcomed him in. "What's up, cuz? Long time no see." I said. We gave each other a warm embrace.

"What's up, muh boy?" He brought about a thousand bags, which he dumped all over me. I led him to my room, so he could get comfortable and so I could get those goddamn cinder blocks off of me.

"So how's things? You still going with Judith or what?" He said while examining my fish. I didn't mention this before, but I have a ten gallon fish tank in my room filled with eight little tropical fish. I've restrained myself from naming them, though. It's not good to name your fish because when they die - and believe me, these little son of a bitches die rapidly - you have to feel bad and all. You practically have to call a pastor and have a memorial service for them or something when they kick the can. That's all too much, if you ask me. I'd rather not name my fish.

"Barely, barely." I said, as I was taking his stuff out of the bags and putting them on hangers. I believe clothes should be respected that way. As soon as you get somewhere, you should immediately unpack your bags and hang your stuff. If you don't, they get all wrinkled and then you either end up looking like some kind of a nomadic vagabond, or you end up not wearing them and that's such a waste.

"What do you mean, 'barely'? What's going on now?" He said, as he completely sprawled all over my bed.

"Arguments. You know, same old crap. Actually we've been avoiding each other like the Black Plague."

"Let me ask you something. Can I ask you something? Seriously." He turned to me with a very earnest look on his face. "You've been having arguments with that girl for as long as I can remember. As a matter of fact, if she isn't consoling you - if she isn't absolutely picking your lifeless self up off the floor - you guys pretty much have absolutely nothing going on. Like, it seems to me - and correct me if I'm wrong - it seems to me, you only need her when you're down and out."

This topic was starting to piss me off. It really was. It was pissing me off mostly because, whenever someone brought it up, I knew that what they were saying made complete sense. I mean, I knew deep down inside that they had a point, but I had no idea why we were still together. "Why don't we talk about this later? What's going on with you?"

"Nothing much. The usual. Drinking, spending time with my girl, joining the Marines -"

I cut him off. "Marines? What do you mean, Marines."

"The Marines. You know, 'The few, the proud, the Marines.'"

"I know what the Marines is. What about the Marines?"

"I joined them, that's what."

I was going halfway out of my skull because he was acting like it was no big deal. He was just laying there like he was talking about some book he had recently read or some new song he just heard. Real nonchalant. "Listen, you're kidding, right? I mean, you're way too calm for someone who just joined the Marines. You know that, don't you? You're way too calm."

"There's no use getting upset about it. It's done. Nothing I can do about it."

"Nothing you can do about it? What in the hell… Did they draft you for Christ's sake? They can't do that, you know. They can't draft you." I was screaming at the top of my lungs.

"Calm down, will you?" He lifted himself off of the bed, walked out of the room and started down the hallway, towards the kitchen, without saying a word. I followed him, breathing like some kind of deranged maniac. When we got to the kitchen, he opened the refrigerator door and began rifling through it. "Where in the hell is your father?" He said, pushing aside some onions and an opened can of Vienna sausages.

"What in the hell does my father have to do with the Marines?"

"Nothing. Where is he?"

"Working, for Christ's sake. Now what in the hell is with this Marines business?"

"Your dad really has to go shopping. This fridge is freaking barren."

"Felix!" I shouted. "The Marines?"

"Well, you know how I signed up for all those colleges? I got accepted to one-" he said, digging into the opened can of the Vienna sausages and pulling one of the last three out.

I interrupted. "That's great, so why don't you go to college?" I was hysterical."

"Can I finish?" He retorted, while holding up the sausage to the ceiling light and giving it a good once over.

I threw my hands in the air. "By all means, finish."

He popped the sausage into his mouth and, while chewing, said, "Thank you. Like I was saying, I got accepted to one. Everything was going good until I got an estimate of my financial aid."

"What'd they give you, half? If they gave you half you could get the whole family to chip in or something."

"Justin, they gave me seven dollars and twenty eight cents."

My head dropped like a hundred pound weight. There was no possible rebuttal for that statement.

"I didn't even tell my mom and dad until after I joined. I didn't want to burden them or anything. I felt like showing them I could make a mature, adult decision. You know, on my own." He said, sullenly, while putting the can of the remaining two sausages back into the fridge.

We stayed quiet for a few minutes. He wasn't feeling too great and neither was I. I couldn't believe that my cousin was going into the goddamn military, in the middle of a war, The Gulf War - Desert Storm they were calling it. It was this whole thing going on in the Middle East. Iraq had invaded Kuwait and we, the United States were going over there to deal with it.

Anyway, he was the only one in the family that I really got to see anymore and now he was going away. It wasn't fair. He was more than just my family, I considered him a real good friend. Now that he was leaving, I started to hate him. I hardly spoke to him for a couple of minutes; but, it didn't last.

Later that night, we found ourselves locked in my room, reminiscing about crazy things in our past. We talked about all the things we had done as kids and how much we both wished we could somehow go back in time. We'd find some kind of crazy time machine - my favorite 'go to' fantasy - and relive our childhood over and over. Maybe we'd even change a bunch of things while we were at it, who knows.

We, Felix and I, had a bang up time when we were smaller, I'll tell you that much for a damn fact. Whether I was over there in Staten Island or he was hanging out up here in the Boogie Down Bronx, we were knocking each other's socks off having a great time. We would take these crazy as hell long walks all the way to Orchard Beach or City Island, which is about three and a half miles away from where I lived, and come up with all kinds of elaborate adventures along the way; either that, or just talk about whatever may have gone on in our lives during the time we were apart. It wasn't bad - the walk. We didn't even notice the thirty minutes it took to get there during the hike. Along the way, there'd be these woodsy trails that made it feel as though you were in goddamn Sherwood Forest. You half expected Robin of Locksley to jump out of one of those trees along with Little John and Friar Tuck and demand all of your money; which was completely fine because we were dirt poor - just a bunch of loose change and maybe a crumpled dollar bill in one of our pockets, so they'd give the money right back to us and we'd be on our merry way. For those of you that have been living under a rock all your miserable lives and didn't get around to reading it, Robin Hood and his ragtag band of cronies robbed from the rich and gave to the poor, amongst a bunch of other really cool stuff. Honestly, it's a timeless classic and you should have read it; if you haven't, you need to put this story down and go read that right away. Sometimes you need to know your priorities. Really.

Anyhoot, as I was saying before I went off in a tangent about the past, Felix got out of the bed, went over to the window, and began to stare out. There was complete silence for a while. Finally, without turning around, he said, "Did I mention my mom and dad were thinking about getting a divorce?" I think he may have been crying at this point, but I'm not entirely sure.

I'm not real comfortable with guys crying. What I mean is, I'm not really sure what to do if a guy starts to cry. If it were a girl, I'd put my arms around her and hold her for a while until she felt better; maybe I'd even try to slip her the tongue to ease her mind. Don't think I'm a dirtbag, I'm just telling you what I've seen a thousand and three times in every movie I've ever watched. There you have a girl, crying her eyes out about something or another, then - out of nowhere - the guy plants a big old wet one on her; she, in turn, reciprocates even more intensely with a passionate display of affection. Trust me, it happens all of the time. With a guy, though, it's a bit more of a tricky, delicate, thing. I mean, what if I put my meat hooks around a guy who's crying and he thinks I'm making some kind of a slick move on him. I'd be mortified. He'd go around school telling everyone that I tried giving him a shot and then I'd have to go into hiding or something crazy like that. You can see my concern about this, so I wasn't exactly certain of what to do at that moment. What I did was, I just sat still and said, "What? No, way. Are you serious? Why?" His parents, my aunt and uncle, splitting up was a complete shock to me because they had been married for about eighteen years and bore three children. I never would have guessed there was anything wrong with them. I thought they were the perfect family and always admired and, quite honestly, envied them.

"They're always arguing about stuff. Stuff that doesn't make sense half of the time. I mean, they've been talking about that crap, divorcing, for years. About six years ago, my father told me that him and my mom weren't going to be together forever. That they were only together because of me, my brother and sister. I felt like telling him to go to hell. I couldn't give two craps about them and their stupid fights." He headed over to his jacket, which was nicely hung up in my closet - thanks to me - and pulled out a pack of Newport menthol cigarettes.

"Since when have you started smoking?" I asked with disbelief.

"I picked it up during the goddamn war. You know how it is with us grunts. Just smokin' and jokin' when we're not layin' down some serious gunfire on the enemy." And with that, he simulated a machine gun with his hands and started making machine gun sound effects, which absolutely tore him up with laughter. As he continued to chuckle, he took a cigarette out of the pack, lit it, took a long drag, held it in - with his eyes closed - and slowly released a plume of smoke into the air.

At that moment I was beginning to understand something. It wasn't extremely clear, but it was helping me to understand what I needed to know about myself. Felix's mom and dad were together a long time. Eighteen years and three kids. I found out now that they've been having problems for years, but they stayed together for the children. The kids, though, didn't seem to be too appreciative of the gesture; so, in a way, it was all a huge waste of time for those two to stay together. Eighteen years of fighting and dealing with each other and knowing that they'd only be separated sooner or later. Subtract a few years and three kids and I was looking at my situation with Judith. I began imagining us in sixteen years, with three children, still arguing and telling our kids that everything they've known was about to come to an end. Everything was now coming to an end for Felix's family, something that could have been avoided without the anguish of squandered time gone by. I was starting to feel sick. I bolted out of the room and into the bathroom to relieve myself. I have a very weak constitution, if you haven't picked up on that little fun fact by now.

SIXTEEN

What occurred in the next hour really blew the top off of the proverbial lid. This is when Rachel, another cousin of mine, called on the telephone. I almost went into a frenzy because of it. It wasn't the call that made me flip, it was the reason in which she called that sent me into hysterics. First of all, as soon as I picked up the phone, she immediately asked for Felix, she couldn't have cared less about me - never even asked how I was doing at all or anything. Secondly, once he got on the phone, I could tell that she was trying to persuade him to leave my place and go see her instead. I couldn't hear what she was saying on the other end; but, I'd hear him reply several times, saying things like, "I wish I could." And, "But that's sort of rude." Then, finally he said, "Let me think about it for awhile."

Here's the worst part. The son of a bitch actually decided to leave. I saw him, shortly after hanging up with Rachel, packing his things. I asked him what he was doing. Without looking at me he said, "I figured I'd go over there, to Rachel's. You know, since I'm going away and all."

My blood pressure must have been completely up to the boiling point at that moment because I started yelling. "You know what? This is insane! What in the hell is wrong with her? If you were at her house, I would never just call you and tell you to leave her!"

The thing of it was, what you should know is, I wasn't yelling at Felix the cousin, but Felix the therapist. Little did that bastard know, he was helping me realize what I needed to figure out about my crummy life. I needed more information, though; more time to put together the missing pieces of the puzzle. Our conversations were serving as some sort of psychoanalysis and our goddamn session wasn't over, yet. Vicariously, through his hardships, I was connecting the goddamn dots to my own insanity. I tried to think of something to say to make him understand. "If you go, that will be totally messed up. I'm like in a mental crisis here and I can't believe you're going to just up and go."

He stopped packing and turned around with a look of bewilderment. "You're in a mental crisis? I've spent the last couple of hours telling you that my world is making a complete hundred and eighty degree turn with my parents getting a divorce and me going away to a goddamn war; and you're telling me you're in a mental crisis?" He let out a breath of utter disgust, shook his head, turned back to his clothes and resumed packing.

I checked myself for a brief moment because I realized how selfish I had come across. I took a few good ol' inhales and exhales and then, with a more tempered tone of voice, I said, "Look, I realize you're going through a lot. I just meant to say that I thought we'd keep talking. I just have a lot going on, too, and I kind of need you."

He just shrugged his shoulders and said, "I know."

"You know? What do you mean, you know? What kind of bastard are you?"

"Hey, just relax, alright? I know it's messed up, but give me a break for Christ's sake. I could get blown to pieces in Iraq and I'd never see her again. And what was I supposed to have said to her, no? "

I absolutely flipped at that. "Goddamn right you say no! You're visiting me for crying out loud. There's a certain kind of etiquette about this sort of thing, you know. There are unwritten rules! You can't just up and do whatever you feel like doing; when you come to visit someone, you don't just leave because someone better calls you! What the hell is so hard about understanding that?"

"Look, like I said, I haven't seen her in awhile and I'm going away soon. What's so hard to understand about that?" He said, never breaking stride with what he was doing.

I was about to tell him what was so hard about understanding that. I was about to tell him how I was reaching a major breakthrough and how he couldn't possibly leave now. I didn't, though. Instead, I walked out of my room and went into the bathroom and closed the door. I felt like punching the crap out of all four of the walls in there. I really felt like it. My adrenaline was really roaring. I started bawling like a newborn who needed his milk and diaper changed. I started crying so hard that goddamn snots started flowing from my nostrils onto my upper lip and my chest felt like it was concaving. I felt this tremendous sense of abandonment and it was tearing me apart inside, along with every other thing that was going on in my life.

I stood in front of the mirror, looking at my pathetic face, full of boogers and tears. A pathetic sight, I have to say. All I needed, to complete the look of shame, was some black mascara to run down my eyes and onto my cheeks. I really did look like one hell of a mess, I'm embarrassed to say. I decided to wash up. I ran the cold water from the sink and began splashing it all over my face. It made me feel better, but not completely.

I could hear that he was in the living room, calling a taxi, when I walked out of the bathroom. I went the opposite way down the hallway and into my room. I sat at my desk, picked up 'Catcher in the Rye" and aimlessly read a few random pages. Whenever I was in any kind of mental, spiritual and emotional peril, I'd peruse through that book, like a parishioner wades through the pages of their bible.

After a couple of minutes, Felix came down the hallway and stood at the entrance of my room door. "Justin, I'm leaving." He stood at the door fruitlessly, waiting - I guess - for some sort of an acknowledgement from me. I'd be damned, though, if I was ever talking to that son of a bitch again. He figured that fact out after about two entire minutes of silent disregard. I heard him, at some point, turn around and head down the hallway and out the apartment door.

My father, who had come home from work sometime throughout all of this, came into my room a few seconds later and asked me what happened.

"It's mutiny!" I screamed. "The soldier's gone AWOL!" I was talking crazy. Absolute madness.

"What in the hell are you talking about?" He said, with a mixed look of perplexity and aversion, most likely due to the tears still trickling down my face.

"I'm talking about Felix jumping to his feet and leaving because Rachel says so." I said, in between the sniffling and chest convulsions. It was, obviously, a hell of a lot more than that; but I knew my audience. You can't go wasting precious thoughts and deep dark feelings on a person who steps on emotions like an eight year old steps on ants while skipping along a sidewalk.

"I hope you're not turning into some kind of queer, crying over guys. I don't have time for that kind of shit." He said, true to form, making an about-face and walking out of the room. "Crying like a goddam little girl. What the fuck is wrong with him?" He said to himself, already half-way down the hall. He wasn't exactly a wealth of support, you know what I mean? What I'm saying is, no one would ever call upon him to talk a suicidal jumper off of the ledge or anything like that.

"Don't worry about me, I'm just fine!" I shouted back. "By the way, how was your day?" With that, I slammed my door closed.

SEVENTEEN

A few days later, Judith and I were on the phone. The Cold War had been adjourned for a short period of time and we were speaking again, here and there; however, on this particular day, it would be the last time we would communicate as boyfriend and girlfriend. It started out very calm, however, with conversations about the weather, TV shows, things like that. All of a sudden, though, things got pretty nasty. Any other time I probably wouldn't mention it because, as you have already witnessed, we argued like mad all of the time. This time, the argument would end our relationship.

After a few minutes of dead air over the telephone, she chimed in and said, "Justin, it's getting late and I have to get up early in the morning."

"What do you mean it's late? It's only ten thirty." She and I used to stay up for hours, sometimes until one in the morning, when things were good between her and I. There were times we wouldn't even say a word for long periods of time; we'd just be on the phone, listening to each other breathe - not in a creepster kind of way, though. It was nice. She'd be glancing through a magazine on her end of the phone and I'd be reading a book on the other. We would comment once in a while on what we found interesting; like, she'd tell me about some glamorous lipstick she wanted to try or some new cucumber diet that interested her and I'd tell her what some character in my book did or said.

Now, all she wanted to do was get the hell off of the phone. "I realize what time it is. I'm just tired, can't you understand that?" She said, vexedly.

"You know, I find myself having to understand a lot of things about you. Except, I don't see you understanding too much about me." This foolhardy and, quite frankly, reckless and very untrue utterance, I realize, was an epic mistake and would lead to absolutely nothing good or remotely productive, but it ejaculated from my stupid mouth like projectile vomit launches from a violently ill person suffering from a stomach virus, nonetheless.

"Jesus, Justin, I just want to go to sleep, that's it. Damn, what the hell is the problem with that?" She was becoming even more irate now that I questioned her decision to hang up.

I was equally, if not more wound up, so I blatantly disregarded her vexation and snapped at her. "You're the problem. Every time I want to talk to you lately, every time I want to spend time with you, you're either not around or you have somewhere else to go. You're the goddamn problem!"

"You know what? Maybe I don't want to be home when you call. Maybe I want to do something else rather than be on the phone with you. Maybe - just maybe - I'm sick and tired of picking your pathetic self up from the ground."

"Oh really? Wow, ok. Why don't you just break up with me if I'm such a problem, huh? What in the hell do you stick around me for if you're so goddam fed up?" Sometimes, when you're really upset, you practically dare the other person to break up with you. I have to tell you, just a bit of friendly advice - you can take it or leave it, don't do this. I mean, unless you're absolutely certain they won't actually call your stupid bluff, just refrain from that kind of thing. It's pretty much relationship suicide. Even if the other person has no intentions whatsoever of breaking up with you, you'll probably end up either getting hung up on or worse. Your significant other will most likely break up with you on general principle, just because you had the absolute nerve to insinuate that breaking up would ruin their life. It's all one big chess match and you really have to know how the pieces move or you'll get your ass handed to you. Just steer clear of that kind of thick headed behavior is the point.

"That's just fine with me! Do you think that's some kind of a problem for me?" Case in point. "Besides, you make me miserable!" She said, with an air of Arctic coldness that would make Lucifer ask for a throw blanket.

CLICK.

This time, surprisingly, I was the one to hang up. I began to cry like a damn baby. I'm almost positive the reason I was crying was because she said I make her miserable. I couldn't stand the sound of it. I knew that, if and when we broke up, I'd be nothing but a bad memory to her; just one gigantic mistake. I could totally picture her with the next guy; they'd be laying in bed, after a magnificent, magical love making session, and she'd tell him how insanely spectacular he is and how her old boyfriend made her so unhappy. She'd go on and on about how very terrible I was and how he, her new man, was so superior to me in every single way.

He'd probably be hung like a large, wild beast, too; just to put the ol' icing on the cake. I'm not doing too well in that department, if you really must know. It's just not something that I'm blessed with in any way, shape, or form. If you've ever played with Barbie and Ken dolls as a kid, and you had occasion to pull good old Ken's pants down, you'd get the idea of what I'm working with down there. If that analogy doesn't make any bells go off in your brain, then just imagine what a frightened turtle looks like. Just go up to a turtle, give him a scare and see what happens to his head; at that point, you'll understand the size comparison to my genitalia. It's just not a thing I'd put on my resume is what I'm trying to tell you.

Anyway, the thought of making Judith miserable made me queasy. I couldn't believe this was happening. I would never have imagined that Jude and I would break up, no matter how bad things got. I guess I took her for granted that way. I assumed she'd always be there no matter what; we'd just stay together and eventually have three kids - two boys and a girl, named Joseph, Joshua, and Josie, live in a beautiful Victorian style house with one of those cliche as all hell white picket fences somewhere in a quiet suburb, and own a dog - a beagle (named Ernest), with brown and black spots - in spite of our tribulations.

My life was making a complete u-turn, back to where I started, back to the fiery pit of hell, in a hurry. I didn't see any reason to go on with anything. She really was my savior, my crutch, my source of oxygen, my clear path in a densely wooded forest - filled with snakes and lions and all kinds of petrifying things. Everything I had done, all that I had accomplished, was because of her. I would be nothing without her. I was losing control over everything and it would only be a matter of time before I would self-destruct.

EIGHTEEN

For the next couple of weeks I became some kind of out of control, pathetic, loser. I'd buy some malt liquor and get drunk out of my mind, even in school, right there in class, which - needless to say - affected my grades to the point that I got these kind of warning letters that my GPA was below 2.0. That's pretty bad. I even started buying bags of weed and smoking it in various staircases and rooftops throughout the Bronx with my old disreputable acquaintances. One night, after about four hours of boozing and puffing herb, I fell asleep in one of those staircases. The gentlemen that were accompanying me had made their exeunt at some point while I napped; so, when the boys in blue arrived - very tall, larger than life and very buffed officers of the law - with nightsticks in hand, I was all by my lonesome. Luckily, they identified me as just some typical strung out loser who posed no immediate threat and let me go on my way. My sluggish appearance – un-groomed, patchy beard; half tucked and half untucked shirt; my hair unkempt and without product (without my Clubman gel and hairspray); and bloodshot eyes - gave me away to anyone who laid eyes on me. I was a disaster.

One day, a few days after the rooftop fiasco, I was walking around the campus in a stupor, dazed on a marijuana high, when I bumped into Emily. "Jesus Christ, Justin, what's going on with you? You look like shit!" She said in sheer bewilderment.

"Thank you." I said with a buzzed chuckle, swaying back and forth and unable to focus on her face.

"Jesus, come on, let's get out of here." She was really concerned. She started guiding me towards the exit of the campus as the other students and professors looked on with shaking heads and looks of repugnance.

"Whatever." I said, stumbling in her arms.

We went to a pizza place a few blocks away from the campus. We found a spot all the way in the back of the place in a secluded corner. She sat me down and propped me up against the wall while she went and bought us a couple of slices of pizza (mine a pepperoni) and two Cokes. As I sat, huddled over the food, Emily was staring at me with a look of despair. The whole time while I was eating like a starved lunatic, she just watched, shaking her ahead in disapproval from time to time. Weed and malt liquor gives you the munchies, if you didn't already know. I must've looked like a real hot mess the way she was gawking at me. "What's happening, Justin? Explain to me what in the hell is going on right now." She finally said, as she clasped her hands and fingers together and placed them against her chin.

I wiped my hands, stained with oil and pizza residue, across my shirt and let out a deep sigh as I placed the last bit of pizza crust into my mouth. The crust is the best part, especially when you let the dripping oil from the cheese and red sauce soak into it; so I tried to savor it. She sat, continuing to leer at me, until I swallowed. "What's the difference?" I said, taking a few long gulps of my Coca-Cola.

"You know, I am your friend. If you have anything you need to talk about, you can talk to me." Her eyes were glossy, as if she were moments away from shedding a tear.

I let out a snicker and began tapping, nervously, on the top of the Coke bottle. I was starting to get really sick. "Judith and me broke up, okay?" I said, finally, not looking in her direction.

"That's no reason to put yourself through this crap. It's not that bad. Nothing in this world is ever that bad."

"Oh, really? I don't think you know what I'm going through. You have no clue what pain feels like, trust me." I started laughing for no reason, but almost instantly stopped and reverted to a stoic, dispirited countenance. I was really wasted. My emotions were running amok, I couldn't control them even if I tried at this point.

"I know more than you realize -" She held back for a second, as if she were debating on whether or not to proceed. She decided to continue, "Artie and I are getting a divorce."

If I weren't so stoned, I'd have been more sympathetic. "Really." I said apathetically.

"Yes, really. He wants to go away, upstate, to Brockport to study sports medicine and he doesn't want me along. He told me he has to move on and that I'm in his way." With that, she got up and put her half eaten vegetarian slice in the garbage (except for some small pieces of crust, which she placed in her jacket pocket) and began to walk toward the door. Then she turned to me, motioned with her head and said, "Come on, let's go."

We went back to the campus and walked around for awhile without saying a word to each other. Although I wasn't feeling entirely better, it wasn't as bad as before. The weather was perfect, it was overcast with a slight chill in the air, and that helped. There weren't too many people around and that was just fine with me. It's nice when you want to take a walk with someone while there's inclement weather just brewing in the sky above and there's no one else in sight. Very cozy. We just walked and what she did was, every few steps or so, she'd feed the squirrels the pieces of pizza crust she saved in her pocket, which was pretty damn thoughtful of her, I must say.

After awhile, we got tired and sat on an empty bench. That's where she turned to me and said, "I want you to know that I've never ignored the feelings you expressed to me. I was just scared to reciprocate them because you're such a valuable friend to me. You never criticize me, you never judge me and I always feel comfortable around you. Hell, I feel more comfortable around you than I do my own husband." She took a breath and continued. "I'm afraid you and I will lose all of that if we were to cross the line and start getting involved. That's why I flipped out that day at your place. I freaked because I see you as someone so very important in my life. Having a sexual relationship would just destroy what good we have. That's what happened with me and Artie. We actually started out as the best of friends before we became a couple. He and I used to be so close, we could talk about anything. Now, I'm lucky if he blinks when we're making love. That's the reason I go out all over the place, it's the reason why I'm always clubbing and hanging out with my friends until all kind of hours of the night." She looked up at the sky, which was now completely covered by black clouds, ready to unleash its wrath upon the earth at any moment. Emily, still looking up, continued. "I don't know, maybe it's me. Maybe I'm the one that messes everything up. It's not like I let him breathe or anything. Every time he turns around, I'm always right there on his heels, for Christ's sake. I never let him alone. I never considered that maybe he has goals and dreams of his own. Maybe it's me. Maybe it's me."

There. Right then and there, as little rain droplets danced on our noses, something magical happened. Something that I had been waiting for since Felix left my apartment that day. My therapy was complete. I finally realized what was going on. Emily, sitting there, looking up at the sky, telling me all her problems, helped me put together the last few pieces of my puzzle. You see, when I met Judith, I was an absolute mess. She helped me find myself; she helped me to stop doing drugs; she helped me get my GED; she helped me get into college; she, essentially, gave me a new life. Like a newborn duckling who becomes his mother's shadow, I attached myself to Jude. She became a necessity; I needed her in order for me to breathe and she knew that, so she was always there.

Little did I realize, though, what she must have been going through. Little did I care to realize that she might want to have a life, too. She might want to strive for greatness and be somebody in this world. She might want to be young and go out with friends and have the time of her life, at an age where you can have the time of your life. She was so young, yet she was not only a girlfriend, but a mother taking care of an eighteen year old. This was unacceptable and I saw it so clearly right then and there.

I don't know why it was so difficult for me to realize this simple idea before. Maybe I didn't want to see it, I don't know. Perhaps when you have someone who nurses you like an infant, your mind gets listless and stops doing for itself. I believe this is what happened to me. I was afraid to think for myself and be with myself and love myself. I realized, at that point, sitting there on that bench with Emily, what I needed to do.

I leaned over to her and gave her a big hug and a kiss on her cheek. "No, you're perfect!"

She hugged me back. "You'll be okay, Justin. We'll be okay. I promise." She said, while straightening out my collar, which was crushed as a result of the hug. Then she put her hand on one side of my cheek and gave me a kiss on the other. "I love you, Justin. Thanks for being my friend."

"No, Emily, thank you for being mine." I meant it, too. Little did I ever care to realize or understand, how valuable her friendship was. I didn't respect the fact, until that very minute, how extremely important a thing like that truly is and that it was right in front of my nose the whole time.

At that moment, the little rain droplets became big rain droplets. The heavens opened up and poured itself upon our faces. We didn't care, though. We just talked and laughed while getting soaked until it was time to go. I can honestly say, those few minutes were some of the best minutes of my life and I will never forget them. I think it may have saved my life. I'm pretty sure of it.

NINETEEN

A few days later, I decided to give Jude a final call. I thought she deserved to know about the conclusion I had come to and about everything I had been thinking; and, she most certainly, I thought, deserved an apology for everything I had put her through for so long.

"Hello, Judith? It's me, Justin."

"What do you want? I'm really busy. I was about to-"

"Look," I interrupted. "I'm not going to take a lot of your time. If you could just give me a few minutes, I'd appreciate it. Just a few minutes, please."

She let out a breath, then said, "A few minutes. I'm really busy."

"Thank you. I won't keep you long. I was thinking a lot about us. I was thinking about all the things that we've done and gone through since we've been together. Basically, the way I figure it, I owe you a huge thank you and a sincere apology. First off, I'd like to thank you for saving me two years ago. I'd like to thank you for staying on the phone with me all those nights and helping me stop using drugs. You helped me get my GED and ultimately get me into college. I owe you a life because you gave one to me. That's my thank you."

"Justin, you really-"

"Wait." I interrupted. "Let me finish. That was my thank you, and now I owe you an apology. After doing all of these things for me, after sacrificing your time, basically your life, for mine, I had the nerve to ask for more. I couldn't turn left unless I called you and made sure it was okay. I didn't know how… I didn't know how to be my own person and I forced you to be my crutch, which you so lovingly did for me. I never let you have your own life, though. While all of your friends talked about fashion and music, their hopes, wishes, and dreams, you were taking care of me, a strung out bum. At sixteen, I gave you the responsibility of an adult, a mother. You didn't deserve that. You spent two years of your life, your high school life, tending to a sickly loser who couldn't take care of or think for himself. Now you're about to go to college; these are the years that you should be finding out who you are. You should be exploring the world and stimulating your mind. Instead, you're wasting your time and life on me. It took me a while to figure this all out, but now I know. Now I know what I did was wrong and I can only offer an apology for putting a stop to your life. I'm sorry. I'm really sorry." I was sobbing a little bit, but I tried for her not to hear it. This wasn't about me, I was able to identify this now; I didn't want my tears to overshadow what I was trying to convey to her, so I tried like hell to hold them in.

There was silence for a bit. I think she was processing the information. I don't think she expected for me to say anything remotely close to what I had just told her. She, most likely, thought the call would be just another bullshit attempt by me to get her attention with some garbage I usually threw her way. The usual melodramatic nonsense that she grew accustomed to flying out of my mouth. Then she finally said, "Justin, you didn't force me to do anything. I made that decision to take care of you on my own. I just… I just got tired. That was my mistake. I could have told you - I should have told you how I was feeling - how I was truly feeling - a long time ago. I'm the one that decided not to. I'm the one that allowed it to go on this long. A part of me was hoping you'd change, that you'd learn to pick yourself up. When that didn't happen, I felt confused and defeated. I didn't know what to do. I guess that's when I began shutting off. Justin, I'm just not ready for that responsibility. I thought I was, but I'm not. I hope you don't hate me because of that. I deserve it, but I hope you don't."

"I don't hate you, Jude. I could never hate you. I owe this new life to you. One day, even if we're not together, I hope I can show you what a great thing you did, what a wonderful person you are to do this for somebody."

"Thank you, babe." She was crying. So was I. This was a pretty emotional moment. Even now, I kind of start tearing up whenever I think about it. Do you blame me? I'm pretty sure you'd feel the exact same way if you were in my shoes. You may not think so, but I'm telling you it's a pretty intense and profound thing to break away from a piece of yourself. It's like cutting off and handing over a finger or one of your damn ears. It's not an easy thing to do.

"Take care of yourself, Judith. If there's any way I can ever help you or do anything for you - to repay you for all that you've done, don't ever hesitate to call. And Jude, I lo -"

"I know. " she interrupted. "Me, too."

"Good bye, Judith."

"Good bye, Justin."

TWENTY

Later that day, I took a long walk on the bicycle path down Pelham Parkway for a couple of hours. It was around seven o'clock in the evening when I found myself thinking about all the things I had experienced during my 'new life.' I thought about Judith; Sweet Sue and Adelphi; Robbing Randy and Looting Larry; Phil and Jerry; Marvin and his goons; I thought of Emily and Selena; and, even Felix. I thought of all these people who played a role in me finding myself again, how the answers were always in front of me, and how I was too wrapped up in my crazy, selfish little world to notice.

As I approached the park, I noticed someone swinging on the swings. It was Selena. I walked over to the playground and right up to her. It was a cool night and the breeze was gently moving her perfectly golden hair back and forth as the swing swayed to and fro like a pendulum. With a slight smile, I said, "Excuse me, little girl." It was what I said to her all those many years ago, when we were little. I told you about it awhile back, in case you forgot.

She sort of smiled back, but said nothing as she continued to swing.

"Listen, Selena -"

She interrupted. "You don't have to explain anything to me, Justin. I mean, if you feel that you have to-"

"Wait a second. I'm not going to explain anything." I paused. "Well, maybe I am, but I want you to listen, anyway." I waited for half a second, expecting to be interrupted, but I wasn't, so I continued. "That night, the night we last spoke, I wasn't ready to hear what you had to say. The problem was me. I knew everything you were telling me was true, but I didn't want to admit it - or I wasn't prepared to admit it. I was in denial. I know now, you were right. Everything you said was right." I stopped to glance at the sky and inhaled the crisp, fresh air. The moon was full and the stars were shining brightly. It was beautiful and perfect. I looked back into her eyes, those translucent, sparkling blue eyes, which were still steadily fixed on me, and continued. "I've been busy trying to find myself and I've finally accepted who and what I am, and I know what I need to do to begin to fix it. I'm going to work on it, I really am. I'm going to learn to love myself and, maybe - somewhere down the line - I can truly, hopefully, share that love with someone else."

She gazed at me for a few seconds more, then, slowly, put her lips on mine, and we began to kiss - delicately, but quite passionately I must admit. Afterwards, still embracing me, with the most brilliant, captivating and most gentle and genuine smile, she said, "That was for luck. You know, with your new life."

I leaned my head back to take her all in. As I beheld her beauty, I wondered if I could ever possibly truly love someone other than Judith. I was wondering if that were ever possible because, one day, I'd like to be in love again. I knew, though, at that moment, I couldn't be. I had too much work to do rebuilding myself. I needed to get reacquainted with myself and it wouldn't be fair to Selena, or anyone else for that matter, to start something in which I couldn't commit.

Selena noticed my stare. "Why are you looking at me that way? What are you thinking about?" Her voice sounded so heavenly and comforting. She looked so beautiful. I wanted to tell her just how perfectly stunning I thought she was. I almost did, too; that is, until I changed my mind. I didn't want to ruin anything by speaking. Sometimes words, any words, can spoil it for two people who are looking up at the stars. Maybe I'd tell her a little later, I'd tell her that she was a gorgeous person - inside and out; I'd tell her how, every time she called me, she brought my spirits up. I'd tell her how much I loved that she was always happy and if I were ever able to love someone else, it would be her. I'd tell her, if I ever got myself together, that maybe she and I could go to a movie together as more than just friends. Perhaps maybe one day. One day, when I have something to offer her, when I can give her as much as she has the power to give me, I will tell her just how very special she is.

At that moment though, I just held onto her a little tighter. I think she understood because she squeezed back. And there we sat, peacefully and quietly under the universe, her head on my shoulder and my arm around her waist, making all of the world's troubles - if but for just a fleeting moment - seem like a single, minuscule grain of sand on a distant, uninhabited island.

TWENTY ONE

I never got to tell Selena any of that stuff, about how I felt for her - at least not at that moment in time. I would love to tell her, though. One day, down the road… maybe. We do keep in regular contact, though. She is, if you care to know, doing extremely well at Mount Saint Vincent. She ended up not failing any of her classes; on the contrary, she got all A's that past semester. She's actually majoring in journalism now and wants to be a writer. I am, incidentally, so very proud of her. I know she is going to be successful in life. Maybe, one day, in between her journalistic writing, she'll compose the 'Great American Novel.' She's got it in her - to be a success - that's for sure.

The reason for not telling her how I felt then was, I arranged to leave New York City to stay with my mother in Georgia, indefinitely. I was leaving New York because I needed a break from it all, if you want to know the truth. I was kind of drained and burnt out. I needed a break on neutral ground, somewhere I didn't know anyone and they didn't know me. It's pretty hard to start over fresh when you have a bunch of people who know all about you hanging around. It's easy to fall back into a rut that way, so I needed a clean slate, a blank canvas if you will. Also, I figured, since I got through my sophomore year of college - albeit by the skin of my teeth - I'd take a break for a year. I'd get my life organized and, once I did, I'd see what I would do from there.

I never got a chance to say goodbye to my cousin before he left for the Marines, but that wasn't because I was leaving for Georgia. What I mean is, I tried calling him up once or twice, but he never called me back. I have to admit, I was pretty upset about that, about him not calling back and all. You'd think he'd be over that by now. Boy, some people can really hold grudges. I did hear, through various family sources, that he was doing well in Iraq - as well as someone can possibly do when they're getting shot at all hours of the day and wondering if they'll make it home alive. I kind of say a few prayers for him everyday to come back home safely. Maybe you could do the same; although you don't personally know Felix, he's sort of fighting for your freedom, so perhaps you could just take a few seconds out of your day to say a few words for him. I'm sure he'd appreciate it.

Emily and I promised to keep in touch. She gave me her mailing address and I gave her my mom's. We promised to write every week and to stay current with each other. The last letter I received from her, she wrote that she and Artie did, in fact, split up. He went up to Brockport where they have this well-to-do sports medicine program. She's doing ok, though. She officially declared herself an English major and she decided that she wants to be an elementary school teacher. She says she's going to get her crazy Master's Degree when she's done at City College, get a job at an inner city school and become Ms. Soto. That's pretty damn cool, if you ask me. I'm honestly very happy for her. I just hope she doesn't have to teach music. That'd be sort of a disaster.

I never spoke to Judith again, nor have I heard from her. I only heard, from mutual acquaintances, that she ended up going to Syracuse University; but other than that, no one knows much else. Maybe we'll pass each other one day in the street and say hello, but after reading Juliana's letter for the hundredth time, which, by the way, all made sense to me now, I knew everything would be okay. You remember the letter; it's the one that I was reading while sitting on the bench at City College that day; the one I folded up and put in my pocket and told you I'd talk about later. I will now keep my promise and produce that letter to you, as it is now apropos:

Dear Justin,

I received your letter today and I must say, I feel like hanging myself. You have to be the most morbid person in the entire world. I don't particularly enjoy knowing that you feel the world is - how did you so eloquently word it? "A lonely waiting room for the afterlife." Why don't you join a club or even a fraternity? You shouldn't just sit on benches, by yourself, writing letters to me. Don't get me wrong, I enjoy hearing from you; it's just that you'll never make new friends or experience the wonderfully sublime things this world has to offer that way.

You remind me of my dear Robert. Ever since he's graduated from NYU, he feels this sort of emptiness, like he's all alone or something. I keep telling him that he simply needs to get adjusted and adapt to the new chapter in his life. He really needs to move on. Really, Justin, moving on is a very natural part of human nature. Caterpillars become butterflies, Justin, they really do. You're like a soul that hasn't accepted its detachment from the body after death. It just wanders around in purgatory, wondering what in the hell is going on, instead of getting its ass up to the pearly gates. You have no idea that your life has just begun. Carpe Diem, my dear little cousin. Seize the day!

To paraphrase Mr. William Ernest Henley, you are the master of your fate: you are the captain of your soul! The dark part of your life is over now. You need to realize that. Your life starts today! Move on, Justin. Move on to bigger and better things. Experience all the beauty there is out there. Explore, write… whatever! Just don't sit around and become a fossil. You've got a whole life to live and before you know it, you'll be old and pruned and it will be too late. Travel the world damn you, see what the globe has to offer. Just don't forget to send me a lousy t-shirt or postcard or something, okay? I love you, Justin. I know everything will be alright. Take care and write me again, soon.

-   Juliana

I folded the letter and put it back in my jean jacket pocket. I thought about it for awhile, standing on the cheese line at Penn Station, waiting to buy a train ticket, but honestly it was the view of the shrinking Manhattan skyline, as the Amtrak Train traveled southbound to Ray Charles' *sweet and clear as moonlight through pines* Georgia, that made me decide to tell this story. I mean, at the very least, just in case this goddamn thing derails, I'd want the rescue crew to have something to read while they're on their crummy lunch break.

END

ABOUT THE AUTHOR

JL Caban was born in the year of Elton John's 'Rocket Man' (1972) to Joe and Lisa in a Mount Sinai hospital room in New York City and grew up in the boro of the Bronx. True to the iconic song, he has always found himself reaching for the stars. Having a keen interest in the literary arts, he found himself reading the works of classic novelists such as Hemingway, Wharton, Bronte and the like and dreamed of one day writing his own page turner. He attended Lehman College where he received a Bachelor of Arts in Psychology, with a minor in English Literature, and a Master of Science in Education; in addition to becoming a Brother of Kappa Alpha Psi Fraternity, Incorporated. JL then went on to teach English to an inner city school in the Bronx before joining the New York City Police Department, where he has achieved the rank of Sergeant. Caban is married to his wife Cecilia and together they have a beautiful baby boy, Julian Lincoln Caban. He is also the proud father of his daughter, Ashley Angelique, as well as his two sons, Jesiah and Joey.